LIGHTER

A. Aduma

A NineStar Press Publication

www.ninestarpress.com

Lighter

© 2021 A. Aduma

Cover Art © 2021 Natasha Snow

Edited by Elizabetta McKay

This is a work of fiction. Names, characters, places, and incidents are either the product of the author's imagination or are used fictitiously. Any resemblance to actual persons living or dead, business establishments, events, or locales is entirely coincidental.

All rights reserved. No part of this publication may be reproduced in any material form, whether by printing, photocopying, scanning or otherwise without the written permission of the publisher. To request permission and all other inquiries, contact NineStar Press at the physical or web addresses above or at Contact@ninestarpress.com.

Printed in the USA

ISBN: 978-1-64890-189-8

First Edition, January, 2021

Also available in eBook, ISBN: 978-1-64890-188-1

WARNING:

This book contains the depiction of a family member hospitalized for a minor stroke; description of domestic abuse of a family member (off-page); child abandonment; grieving; and depictions of underage teenagers smoking marijuana.

After a bad breakup, Rasheed is determined to spend his last year of high school focused on his course work and to finish it with as little drama as possible. But when disaster strikes and his grandma ends up in the hospital, the threads holding his life together start to slowly unravel. Now, Rasheed has to deal with the return of his absent mother and sharing a home with her despite their strained relationship.

With old hurts surfacing and family dynamics shifting, Rasheed finds comfort and humor from his best friends, the Herman twins he's tutoring, and his crush, Adam Herman, who's not as unavailable as Rasheed had once thought. With more time spent together, Rasheed finds his feelings for Adam may never have gone away. And the feelings may not be as one-sided. Except, Rasheed has to confront old mistakes and come to terms with his own issues first, and a relationship may just complicate everything.

To my brain cells, both alive and dead, you put up a brave fight. You can rest now.

Chapter One

"Please tell me it's *mahamri*," I said enthusiastically when I saw Granma kneading dough that would hopefully be rolled, cut into little squares, dipped into deep frying oil, and covered in whipped cream to create a slice of heaven. Paired with hot chai, it opened the door to another dimension.

Granma pounded the dough, one-two, and flipped it over. "It is."

"Should I start on the tea?"

"You should start by taking the trash out." She straightened, wiped the thin film of sweat from her forehead, and pointed to the overflowing trashcan. I could have emptied it last night, but I had an assignment due and each second counted; the four minutes it would have taken had seemed like a lifetime.

"Okay." I stepped farther into the kitchen and pinched some of the dough. Granma smacked my hand with her flour-covered one. I should have seen it coming; it was a dance we'd been doing since I was five—I'd pinch the dough, she'd slap my hand, and warn me about worms making my stomach swell.

Sure enough she said, "*Tumbo lako litafura.*"

I refrained from rolling my eyes. The way she used to tell it, when I was a kid my stomach would get as large as a balloon before it burst, spraying worms everywhere.

I tossed the dough in my mouth, grabbed a pot, filled it with water, and put it to boil for tea. One thing Granma and I liked was tea—tea in the morning, tea in the afternoon, tea before bed—and coming to America hadn't changed that. As soon as she was done with the *mahamri*, she'd set herself up on her favorite floral armchair in front of the TV with her cup of steaming hot tea and catch up on some daytime soaps. Sometimes I joined her—TV dramas had some really cute guys.

"They finally gave up the dog," Granma announced.

"Huh?"

"Mrs. Kyle and that dog. The *pepo chafu* will not be terrorizing us again."

Mrs. Kyle lived on the other side of the street, one house down from us. Her bulldog, Teddy—a name that maybe shouldn't be handed out so easily to slobbering dogs—had the bad habit of chasing and attacking people, and she refused to put it on a leash. Granma did not like her. The whole neighborhood didn't like her.

"Paul was right," she continued, "Soon as someone threw in the word 'sue,' she became more accommodating."

There'd been a lot of that lately—Paul this and Paul that. It would have slipped my mind if I hadn't noticed her FaceTiming him two weeks before, and then a day ago. Paul only lived a fifteen-minute drive away, so why not text? Anyway, what was so important that she needed to video call?

"I'm guessing some are for Paul?"

"Yes."

"That's nice."

She pulled a drawer open and retrieved a rolling pin. "Why are you saying it like that?"

"How am I saying it?"

"Like you mean to say something else."

"It's nothing— Okay, you and Paul are...friendly," I teased.

"I don't have many friends; another one never hurts."

"True, but I don't know many people who go around fixing other people's houses out of the kindness of their heart."

Granma fixed her eyes on the dough and started to roll it. "It's called kindness. Looks like you've forgotten the meaning of the word."

"I remember," I said quickly before it turned into a speech about *undugu*. Yes, yes, love thy neighbor, unless it was Mrs. Kyle, of course. Lines had to be drawn somewhere.

I added a cinnamon stick and some ginger into the pot and turned to head back to my room. Granma pointed to the trashcan. "*Usitume nikwambie mara ya pili.*"

Right, the trash. I sighed.

Her eyes bored into me as I bent to pick it up, which usually made me more self-aware. Like, had I brushed my teeth or cleaned my room? "I don't know where your mind is nowadays."

I paused. "Just tired." Second week of school, Granma!

I was still trying to shake off summer vibes and find my back-to-school rhythm. It wasn't going great. On top of the mound of piling homework and the early waking hours that turned me into a zombie—sometimes even with growling, and on really bad days, I could bite someone's head off—I was trying to dodge Scott, my ex-boyfriend. Whenever he weaved his way into my thoughts, my chest would burn with shame, and my body would turn into a bundle of nerves. That chai and *mahamri* better come quick. I needed a pick-me-up.

"You put your shirt on backward on Tuesday and didn't notice."

"My mind was elsewhere."

Her eyes narrowed. "And you're not on drugs?"

I refrained from sighing. "No, I am not on drugs."

"What is it, then?"

"Not enough sleep."

Apologize, a voice echoed in my mind. Apologize? As in, like, say sorry and stuff? Hmm.

Not that I hadn't thought of it before, but how did people do that? The idea sounded foreign. Save for when I stepped on someone's foot or bumped into them by accident; that was easy because they *were* accidents. Honest mistakes. What I had done had *not* been an honest mistake. So how did someone apologize for dumbness?

It was easier to stay clear of him, avoid any more drama, and focus on school.

If I ignored it maybe it would have no option but to magically—

"Eedy!" I paused, spooked by how she sounded— like a rusted engine trying and failing to come to life. As I put the watering can down, there was the sound of a body hitting the floor with a soft thud.

My heart leaped into my throat, and my stomach twisted with dread.

I rushed back to the house and found Granma lying on the floor—flat on her stomach and still as a rock. The world tilted and blurred together.

"Granma?" I said in a shaky whisper. I fell to my knees and with weak arms managed to turn her over. My breath caught at the sight of her. Her dark eyes were wide open, unfocused, and unblinking. A chill snaked down my back. I leaned down and felt her warm breath on my face. Oh, thank fuck.

I grabbed her hand and recoiled at its limpness. "Granma, are you okay?" Of course, she wasn't okay.

She groaned.

"*Tafadhali amka!*" Please get up. I tried to pull her up and failed. Granma wasn't small, and despite my size, I couldn't get her to move. My pulse started to race and a heavy weight pressed down on my chest; breathing became difficult. I gasped for breath.

No. No. It would be alright.

"Musa?" she whispered roughly.

The hope I'd been holding on to sank somewhere to my toes. "No, Rasheed. Eedy."

Musa was my *babu*'s name—my grandfather—a man we'd silently agreed to never speak of, ever. To Granma, saying his name was equal to calling on the devil, which wasn't that far off from the truth.

I needed to call for help. She lay on the floor, immobile, her empty stare on me. I did not want to leave her. My eyes blurred. I stood on shaky feet and rushed to get my phone still buried under books from last night's homework rush. My palms were sweaty enough it took a few swipes before I hit dial on the emergency contact. The person on the other end promised the ambulance would be coming soon.

I returned to crouch next to Granma and took her hand. She slurred something unintelligible that I failed to understand. "They're coming." I squeezed her hand.

She grumbled. It sounded like a mangled animal. I blinked to keep the tears from falling, but that only made them fall harder.

"Itsfine," she slurred. Her hand twitched in mine.

It didn't seem fine.

Last time she had ended up in hospital, it hadn't been fine. Three weeks after I turned eight, and the world had turned upside down. I fought off the gnawing helplessness and tried to cling to positive thoughts. It would be alright.

Granma would be alright.

She didn't really have a choice. She had her dramas waiting for her, Christmas was a few months away— Granma loved Christmas, all those sales and store decorations hyped her up—and I was going to graduate from high school.

Chapter Two

Signs of a stroke.

The paramedic's words echoed in my mind. A stroke. The little knowledge I had of strokes stemmed from watching TV. My mind conjured an old person, seated in a wheelchair unmoving, sometimes with a hand that twitched.

My gut knotted painfully. The idea of Granma spending the rest of her life in a wheelchair broke my heart. Granma was an energetic person, she laughed with her whole body and loved to sing and dance—she always made sure her church clothes were lose enough to allow for easy movements during praise and worship, and she walked like there was an invisible beat playing in the background.

It didn't make sense. How could this have happened? It had been a normal Saturday: I'd started out on my laptop, rewarding myself with fanfic after completing my assignment, and when I heard Granma moving about in the kitchen, I'd kicked off my blankets, eager to see what she was up to. It ate at me, how that had turned into waiting in the hospital hyperacute wing as Granma went through scans and tests to tell if it had been a stroke, and what kind.

She'd been fine, and then she wasn't.

My knee hadn't stopped bouncing, and my stomach was a tangled knot. Every time the word stroke came to mind, I thought I'd hurl for sure.

The doors swung open, and a nurse with red hair stepped into the hallway. Her eyes landed on me. I tensed waiting for her to approach and tell me something had gone wrong. But her gaze moved past me to the man furiously typing on his phone seated across from me.

Fuck.

I imagined in another universe, Granma's voice hadn't been strangled and missing her whimsical Swahili accent, and instead of a cry for help, she'd been calling on me to check on the boiling water. In another universe, she'd have finished cooking, I would have finished making tea, we would have had our breakfast. I would have gone to work, leaving her on the couch in front of the TV, and probably have found her there when I returned. In her words, a perfect free day.

Now, I had to text Mrs. Clay and tell her I wouldn't make it. I helped Mrs. Clay with gardening and yardwork since her arthritis had worsened, making kneeling and bending difficult. She, instead, would sit on her porch, wearing a gigantic hat and dictating every move I made, from how I held a shovel to how I could look at her—not with wide eyes which unfortunately was the only state my eyes knew.

While I was at it, I needed to tell Mo and Peep that Granma was in the hospital. Natalie, too...and Frida. I didn't have the energy to do it. It would make it all too real. I was still waiting to wake up and find drool on my physics textbook.

I managed to pull out my phone and find Mrs. Clay's number. I started to type. *Hello Mrs. Clay. I'm really sorry, I won't be able to make it today. My grandmother was rushed to the hospital.* I hit send.

The door opened again. I looked up, tensed, but it was someone entering not leaving. This wait was slowly killing me. If I waited any longer, they'd have to find me a sick bed.

My phone buzzed. *Rasheed, how many times has your grandmother been sick?*

Right. That. I'd probably used the excuse of Granma being fictitiously sick so I could skip work a little too often because a day of the sun beating down on me while she pointed out my mistakes held less appeal than staying in and watching TV with Granma. And it was only twice. In both cases, Granma had said something about migraines.

Granma's superstitions lodged themselves in my mind. What if I'd brought this on her by lying about her health?

No, it couldn't be.

I took a picture of the waiting room and sent Mrs. Clay the picture. *It might be a stroke.*

There was a long pause as I watched the three type dots. I held my breath. Mrs. Clay was a little bossy. Completely understandable, if I ever lived to be seventy-seven, I would be too. But she paid me, and I didn't have to ask for money from Granma all the time. I didn't want to lose her as a customer.

Finally, the message appeared. *Sorry to hear that. How is she doing?*

I filled her in on the situation, and she wished Granma a quick recovery, and that her yard would be waiting for me after things calmed down. Oh, thank fuck.

Finally, a short round lady in a white coat approached me. She had heavy lidded bloodshot eyes and a tooth gap. "Are you Rasheed Tawi?"

I nodded, too numb to speak. She introduced herself, but it went over my head. She explained some other things that seemed irrelevant. Did Granma have a stroke or not? Was she alive? Please tell me she was alive. My mind whirled trying to catch and make sense of the words falling out of her mouth in her soft toneless voice. I nodded again, hoping that would make her get to the point faster.

Finally, I caught on—a "ministroke" with temporary effects.

"So she's okay? She's awake?"

"Yes, she's awake." The woman's lips stretched into a tired smile. "I'll take you to her."

I heaved a sigh of relief.

*

Granma had her eyes closed when I entered the room. A nurse with a double chin was putting pillows under her left side. I approached her bedside with timid steps. She seemed to sense me hovering and blinked before her dark eyes settled on me. They were sunken, dull and watery. Her skin more wrinkled than I remembered. It occurred to me Granma was not young—even worse, she was growing old. She was fifty-nine about to hit the big six-o.

My eyes stung with tears. "You good?" I asked. Through a tight throat.

"Feeling hazy."

I swallowed, my throat itchy and dry. "I thought..." I tilted my head up to keep the tears from falling. It was difficult to utter the D-word; I couldn't risk the grim reaper trolling the hospital hallways, hearing it, and come knocking on Granma's door.

She patted my hand. "I'm good now; God has been kind." Her speech was slurred and her voice low.

I collapsed on a chair and tightly wrapped my fingers around its arms to stop them from trembling.

Another doctor joined us to tell us more about the results of the scans and tests. I tried to settle my mind and somehow catalogue the events of the day, filter out the fear, and replace that with a bit of logic and rationality. The doctors called it a "transient ischemic attack." The temporary effects often resolved themselves, but they encouraged a surgery to help minimize the occurrence of an actual stroke. What I got was: Granma was fine. She'd get to do all the dancing she wanted, and the world wouldn't be denied her rhythmic walking style. They explained a little bit more about the surgery and left.

"I hope," Granma started then paused and licked her lips. She pointed to the glass of water with a straw. "Water." I held the glass as she drunk and then put it back down. "I hope you didn't leave the stove on."

"I didn't."

"Are you sure?"

"Yes." In between the paramedics trying to figure out what Granma's problem was and me looking for appropriate shoes, I'd remembered to turn the stove off as the last drops were about to evaporate.

"We need a house to go back to." She sighed and sank further into the pillows. "But the dough, that's definitely wasted. I'd been so excited about making *mahamri*."

"When you're well, you can make it again," I told her. "I can assure you I am not thinking about the ruined dough."

She sighed again. "Who'd have thought the day would end with me in the hospital?"

Definitely not me.

"Did you call Frida?"

"Not yet."

"Or Natalie?" I shook my head. "Paul?" I furrowed my eyebrows. "Not even your friends?"

"I'll call them." First, I had to make sure you were not dying.

Granma stared at me expectantly.

I pulled out my phone. Phone calls exhausted me. I preferred texting, face-to-face, or nothing—depending on my mood. I found the group Mo, Peep, and I had created and sent a message. *Granma was rushed to the hospital, she had a stroke.*

I waited for a reply, doubting one would come soon. Peep had gone over to his girlfriend Tani's place. Her parents were out, and I doubted Peep had his attention fixed on the phone. Mo always had his notifications turned off and could take either a minute or a week to reply.

"Texts?" Granma said disapprovingly.

"We talked about this."

She shook her head. "Give me that phone."

Reluctantly, I handed it over, grateful I hadn't started the day by exercising my right hand and, therefore, nothing on the phone would make Granma possibly lose her eyesight. She dialed Frida first. The phone rang and rang; no one picked up. Not a surprise. She'd probably gone into a state of shock at seeing my name on her screen. Or she didn't have my number; maybe that would explain her lack of texting or calling. It was possible she was asleep—she *was* in Afghanistan shooting a documentary on their Independence Day celebrations—but I doubted it. Devils never slept.

Granma had me type up a message.

Natalie Herman picked up on the second ring. From where I sat, I could make out her startled high-pitched voice as Granma delivered the news. She was Granma's best friend, her only close friend. They'd met in the grocery store when Granma had been trying to figure out what "oz." meant. Not like it mattered, but Granma was the type to read instructions and ingredients, even on toothpaste. They discovered they were both new to town. Natalie had a tenured position teaching gender studies at Albert Bernard University. Her mother was Tanzanian, but she'd been born and raised in California. By the time they made it to the checkout counter, they'd decided they were best friends, and I was being invited for a playdate with her son, Adam Herman, who happened to be in the same grade. Their friendship had grown over the years while Adam and mine had withered and died.

Paul's call went unanswered. She frowned at the screen before she handed back the phone and asked me to type another message.

"Okay," I said as I stood and stretched, my whole body stiff from exhaustion. "I'll be back."

"*Unaenda wapi?*"

"To the bathroom. I don't have to announce that."

"Oh." Granma's lips twitched, and her eyes shone with amusement. I smiled back, assured things would look up.

*

I cringed when I saw myself in the mirror. Painted on my face was the rollercoaster of the morning I had ridden. My eyes red and puffy, my lips cracked and flaky, cheeks streaked with dried tears, and hair unkempt. I splashed water on my face, ignoring that in an hour or two I'd be ashy.

As I dried off, my phone belted out Tupac's "Dear Mama." The ringtone was a joke—Frida was my mama, but she was *not* dear. I braced myself. "Hallo?"

"Rasheed? It's Frida." I pinched the bridge of my nose. "How's Mama doing?"

"She's fine now. She fell, and I had to call the ambulance." I'd seen an ambulance called once when Peep broke his arm, bone sticking out and white flesh exposed. "It was—it was pretty scary." I wished she was here with me. It was a dumb wish.

I recounted what the doctors had said, and at the word surgery, she inhaled sharply.

"Can I talk to her?"

"I'm not with her right now; I'll ask her to call."

"Okay." There was a long pause. I tapped my finger on the counter. "I'll see if I can get a flight and come home."

I blinked. It had been six months since I'd last seen Frida, but it didn't count, not when she would be here today and gone by tomorrow. I hated it. As a kid, it'd been nerve-racking waiting for a mother I hadn't seen in months as she shot her documentaries, only to see her for a week or two before she left again. By the time I was fifteen, my patience had worn off because even if she did have to work, she could have called or sent an email or text. There was no excuse for her ignoring me. "Aren't you working?"

She sighed. "Not currently, no."

"Oh?" If she wasn't working, why hadn't she come home? I paused, waiting for her to explain herself.

"I'll be there as soon as I can."

"Okay." Despite myself, I sagged with relief. If Frida came home, she would take some of the load off. She would know what to do. She would put things in order. Then, as soon as she was done, she'd be off again.

After the call ended, I spent a few extra minutes replaying the conversation in my mind. Something niggled at me.

Frida hadn't asked how *I* was doing.

Chapter Three

Paul Obare walked into the hospital room with all the urgency of a desperate man. He paused in the doorway, his gaze raking over Granma as he took a slow and careful catalogue of her from head to toe before settling on her face and exhaling loudly. He stepped further into the room. He was panting, had a thin sheen of sweat on his bald head, and wore a wounded expression as if someone had stolen his candy.

In two strides, he was by her bedside. "Rukia!" He cupped her face, tilted it up, and scanned it as if he had X-ray vision or something. My eyes bulged, almost falling out of their sockets. "Oh thank God you're alright!"

Granma's cheeks had gone impossibly round, and her eyes bounced around the room before they settled on his. "Uh, Paul, yes...I am fine."

Paul rubbed a thumb over Granma's cheeks before he let go. I choked on air. What was happening?

"Hey, Rasheed. How are you doing?" Paul asked gently.

"Hi," I squeaked. "Um, well...you know." What was he asking? And why had he touched Granma like that?

"I'm sorry I didn't pick up. I was doing some sanding."

"You're here now," Granma said.

He squeezed her hand and sat on the edge of the bed. I turned to Granma to see her reaction; she was beaming like a ray of sunshine.

Heat crawled up my neck. This was weird. I was caught between wanting to roll around on the floor laughing because this shit was absurd, and leaving because this was, like, super weird. I took door number two. I was hungry anyway, starving; the last time I'd eaten was last night.

"I'm going to look for food," I announced and narrowed my eyes when I got no response. I cleared my throat. "Want something?"

"Great idea," Granma said. She glanced my way.

"Do you want something?" I said more forcefully.

"Oh. No."

In the cafeteria, I bought myself a tuna sandwich and found an empty table. I set the bottle of water down with too much force as I took my seat, my mind still in the hospital room. What had I witnessed? Paul and Granma acting like—like a couple. I'd known there was something there, but I hadn't been aware it was like that. Like, that affectionate. How could I have missed it?

I frowned as I thought back to their interactions. Paul and Granma met last year during a Jamhuri Day barbecue in Dallas, put together by a Pastor Mwaura. Granma had dragged me along, and for the sake of keeping up a festive spirit, she'd played a mixture of *zilizopendwa* and Taarab for a solid three hours on the way. By the time we got to the party, my energy reserves were low.

The party had been boring. There'd been one person my age, and of course, she was an introvert. Paul introduced himself to Granma when he heard her complain about how difficult it was to find an affordable repairperson to fix our loose kitchen cupboards. Paul was a woodworker who did a bit of carpentry on the side, and he lived in Brooksville. Of course, we did too. There were close to two thousand of us Africans working for the pharmaceutical company there. A week later, Paul was fixing stuff in our house. A few months later, Granma was including him in our meal plans.

I reached into my pocket and pulled out my phone. It was on silent mode to piss Frida off if she called back. (How could she not have asked how I was? It was basic decency.) Sure enough, she'd called several times before she gave up and left a message. *I might be able to get back by Monday. I hope nothing has gone wrong. Call me.*

There were also missed calls from Mo, Peep, and Tani, the messages all echoing the same sentiment: is she okay, send address, pick up, are you okay? I wiped the grease off my hands and typed back a reply, catching them up and ending with *I'm doing okay*. Better than before at least. My heart rate had slowed, and I could hear myself think.

We want to come see her, Peep announced.

We can bring lots of sugar. Mo added a sunglasses emoji.

I smiled. Peep and Mo were my people. I'd met Peep through church, back when I went to church, and Mo through Peep. We were a unit, sometimes a functioning one, other times, we shared a single brain cell.

It was a good offer. I was easy; give me lots of candy, and we were solid. It was a tempting offer, but being around people after the day I'd had seemed like a chore. I wanted to sleep. I deserved sleep.

ME: *Come tomorrow. It's late and I want sleep.*

Mo sent peace sign emojis. *Alright, see you then.*

PEEP: *I'll come after church*

MO: *also going to church btw...*

ME: *why?*

PEEP: *Malia...*

I raised my eyebrows. Mo had an unhealthy relationship with Malia. Mo liked Malia, had even asked her to date him more than once. She'd said no both times but still kept Mo close by, in case she needed a box of tampons at the butt crack of a Sunday morning or wanted a cute ring or two from her favorite jeweler.

MO: *no lectures. It's serious this time, we're going slow.*

Does that actually work? Ever?

Peep must have been reading my mind because he replied with, *read as "not going anywhere"*

Mo sent middle fingers, and I knew that was the last we'd hear from him until tomorrow. I needed to head back too. I texted Peep goodbye, grabbed the trash, dumped it, and made my way through the hallways to Granma's room.

*

Natalie Herman was there when I got back, seated on what I now referred to as "my chair"—wow, I had claim to a hospital chair. She was an average-sized woman with almond-shaped eyes, deep brown skin, and dimples that could hold water. She wore a white skirt with a cream-colored silk blouse, looking like she'd stepped off a runway.

Natalie pulled me into a hug the moment she saw me. She was a hugger, always had been, and it was unfortunate she'd passed her tendency for physical affection on to Adam who'd let his hand rest on my thigh on numerous occasions, always had an arm swung around my shoulders, and smiled too damned much. How was I to know he didn't mean it like *that* when I hadn't been used to such physical intimacy before? Thinking back on those memories always caused ripe embarrassment.

She pulled back and patted my shoulder. Her tone was soft and kind; it made me want to burst into tears and cling to her for comfort.

"You should have called me immediately."

"I was caught up in everything." I waved at the hospital room.

"Of course. Know you can always call me, always."

My eyes stung with unwanted tears. "Thank you."

"Anytime."

I deposited myself on the other chair in the room and kept busy scrolling through my phone while the grownups talked.

After a while I started to nod off, which was a testament to how exhausted I was as these chairs—stiff, thin cushioned, and an ugly shade of gray—were not comfortable. I twisted a few times looking for a comfortable position but found none because of my long legs. Dammit.

"Are you sleeping?" Granma's dark eyes were not as glazed over, and her speech lacked the sluggishness from before.

"No?" But I wouldn't have minded if someone handed me a bed and this miraculously turned into a vivid dream.

"You definitely were," Natalie said with a knowing smile. She smiled the same as Adam, wide, bright, and with teeth.

"You said something about not getting enough sleep. You should go home and rest."

"I want to stay with you."

Granma shook her head. "No need for you to miss sleep. I'm doing much better. I almost feel like my old self. Besides, you have school on Monday, and you need time to recover."

I frowned. "School?"

"Yes. You thought I'd let you miss school?" She laughed. "Go home and get some sleep; you really look like you need it. You also need to change shirts and a shower."

I was wearing a faded One Direction tee that I would have preferred hell freeze over before anyone saw me in it. There were stains from the spaghetti we'd had on Thursday—eating spaghetti was an art form I had yet to master. Not to mention my armpits were a mess—moist with sweat and sticky—and what little deodorant I'd applied had clearly been overworked.

"You don't have to worry."

I hesitated, thinking back to her lying on the kitchen floor so still and helpless. What if something happened and there was no one to call the nurses and doctors? "I can't leave you alone."

"Paul can stay with me, right Paul?" Granma turned to where he stood by the window stretching his legs.

His whole face lit up, and he watched her with a fondness that washed some of the sleep away and made me alert. "Yes, I can stay." He smiled at her.

I faced Natalie, hoping to see the same confusion reflected in her face. She glanced my way and grinned. Even after six kids, four of them boys, and a dangerous pregnancy with twin girls, she was always sunny and vibrant.

I shrugged. "I guess I could sleep."

"Natalie can drop you off then."

"How about he come stay the night?" Natalie suggested.

I froze.

"That's a good idea," Granma said. "Then he wouldn't be alone."

"He shouldn't be alone."

That's exactly what should happen. I needed sleep and that only required a bed and blankets. Plus, I thought Granma and I had come to a silent understanding that going to the Herman's was no longer an option for me. It was an irrational decision and even the reason sounded dumb playing in my mind. "Thank you for the offer, but I don't mind being alone." I definitely wanted to be alone.

"And what will you eat?" Granma asked.

"I'll microwave the leftover pizza."

"Oh, you should definitely come over. We made lasagna."

I ran a hand over my head. I did like lasagna, actually loved it. The first place I'd ever eaten lasagna was at the Herman's, and it had been finger-licking good, even though I had to fight off the urge to do just that. Natalie always offered me a second helping.

"When's the last time you were over anyway?" Oh, I could point to the date if someone handed me a calendar. "You're always promising to visit but never do."

Natalie wanted me to pay her house calls the way Granma did as if we were friends. I had kind of latched on to her—okay, very much latched on to her. And she'd been kind and not treated me any differently than the way she treated Adam. She would ask how my day was, how I was fitting in, if Adam was looking after me...

Adam. Hadn't hung out with him in forever. Seeing him would be so awkward.

But it wouldn't kill me, and I wasn't fourteen anymore; the grudge was stupid, and I wanted lasagna. "Okay."

Natalie beamed. "Finally, after what? Four years?" Maybe. "You'll get to see how we renovated the pool. You were so attached to it!" I did miss spending summers at their pool. One that wasn't crowded or dirty. "And I bet Adam will be happy to see you."

Doubted that. We were not friends anymore.

"You'll, like, not get sick or anything, right?" I asked Granma as Natalie gathered her things.

"Promise." She opened her arms. "Come here."

I went to her, and she pulled me into a hug. For a moment, I was unsure of how to react until my brain kicked in, and I wrapped my hands around her.

"Make sure you sleep." She pulled away and smacked a wet kiss on my forehead.

"Granma!" I protested.

She cackled. "Be good."

"I'm always good."

Chapter Four

Natalie let me pretend to nap in the car to avoid the how's school questions or her asking why I never went to their place anymore, which she always did. I always told her I was busy, I very well could never tell her the truth: Natalie, your son was too affectionate with me, and I thought it meant more when it did not. A part of me was sure it had been real. Adam got the affectionate part from his mom, sure, okay. But sometimes when our eyes met, I saw the longing I felt reflected in them. I'd been wrong.

The Hermans lived in the newer neighborhood of Brooksville with green lawns, well-maintained driveways, and enough distance between the houses that they didn't have to hear their neighbors in a screaming match.

Natalie ushered me straight to the kitchen, and I was grateful our priorities aligned. The house had changed; the kitchen's cream walls were now a stark, almost blinding, white, and large French doors provided a view of the backyard and pool. I settled on a stool at the breakfast bar.

"Here." Natalie set three large slices of lasagna in front of me. My stomach rumbled in anticipation.

"Thank you."

"And I want it all gone."

No complaints from me. She left to go change from her work clothes, leaving me bathed in complete silence. Their house had never been this quiet. Before, Leo, the second oldest, would play his RnB or old hip-hop at earsplitting volumes when he was home during the school breaks. Izzy, the third born, always had a group of friends over to film stuff for his YouTube channel, which had become sensational over the last few years. Adam, Peep, and I'd had a habit of chasing each other around with toy guns and yelling at each other at the slightest provocation. The twins, laughing or crying. Natalie on the phone. Mr. Herman watching ESPN or the news. Noise everywhere. Now, Leo had moved out, Izzy was in LA, according to his Instagram, and Adam was too old to be playing tag.

The sound of feet slapping against the floor caught my attention. I turned, expecting to see Natalie...

Adam paused in the kitchen entryway, his lips parted as his dark eyebrows pinched together. He stared at me with wide eyes. "Rasheed?"

My gut fluttered. It had been too long since I heard him say my name or been this close without a sea of students between us. "Uh, hey."

"Hey." His eyes stayed on me as he headed for the fridge. I allowed myself to take a casual once-over. His hair was longer, cut into a low fade with tight curls; he now had a smattering of pimples on his cheeks. A fitted black shirt emphasized his broad shoulders and showed off his muscled arms. The only unchanged things about him were his almond-shaped eyes framed by thick, long lashes that matched dark, thick eyebrows, and his lips, still wide and full with a peaked Cupid's bow. Daydreaming about those lips against mine had gotten me through eighth-grade history with Mr. Pratt, who wheezed after every sentence he finished.

Adam looked good.

I became aware of my crusty self in my ratty shirt. Well, it had been a day.

Adam cocked his left eyebrow when our eyes met.

Heat crawled up my face. I fixed my eyes on my plate.

"Sorry about your grandmother," he said quietly.

He held a can of Coke in one hand while the other fiddled with its top. The softness of his words roused fear.

"Thanks."

I tried to push the fear away only to open the door for doubt to creep in. Would she be okay? She'd been doing fine ten minutes before she fell, and the doctors had mentioned the probability of another stroke. I should have stayed. Leaving her alone had been a stupid idea.

Adam's fingers stopped tapping. "I'll..." He pointed to the staircase, situated off the kitchen.

I nodded, and he left. I should have gone home and taken Mo and Peep up on their offer and let them come to me, or I could have gone to them.

I sighed and spooned more lasagna into my mouth. As Granma liked to say, *kukiwa na shida, kula kwanza.* If there is a problem, eat first.

Natalie came back, her head in a satin scarf and wearing a *dera,* a loose cotton dress with brown-and-yellow tie-dye that Granma had gifted her. "Let's get you to bed; you must be tired."

"I am."

We went up the stairs and down a hallway lined with photos of all the Hermans: Wally, the eldest, playing soccer at an early age; the twins in matching outfits; Adam on his fifth birthday; Izzy holding up a camera; Leo graduating college; Natalie receiving an award; Mr. Herman holding up a certificate. The door to Leo's room now had a small chalkboard on it with the writing, "I said I was SORRY" instead of the Lil Wayne poster from before. Adam's room was at the end of the hallway.

We stopped at his door, and Natalie announced she was coming in before she pushed it open. The room hadn't changed much—the same twin beds, one for Izzy, the other for Adam, and Spiderman posters on Adam's side, and a shelf for his action figurines. As usual, Izzy's side was neater, with zero posters and a shelf carefully stacked with electronic equipment while Adam's had an unmade bed piled with clothes and books. A large desk with a PC separated the beds, and Adam sat at it with a headset on, the screen paused on an RPG with a Viking setup.

"Jesus Christ, Adam. Don't tell me you've been on that chair since I left," Natalie chastised with a sour look on her face.

"Nah, I only fired it up again..." His lips twitched.

Natalie arched her eyebrow at him—the eyebrow arch was a Herman thing, and they did it gracefully because they had beautiful thick dark eyebrows with a natural curve.

Adam was lying, even I could tell that. But Mrs. Herman let it go with a look that said—for now. "Rasheed is here," she said, announcing the obvious.

"Yeah, we met downstairs."

"Oh," Natalie seemed a bit disappointed. She turned to me. "You'll take Izzy's bed." She pointed to the one with navy bedding. "The sheets are clean, right Adi?"

"Yeah, they're clean."

"And you put a toothbrush in the bathroom."

"Yup, and fresh towels." He swung his chair from side to side.

Natalie eyed him suspiciously.

"I did, Ma, promise."

"You remember where everything is?"

I nodded. "Yeah."

She studied me. "Try and sleep, it will be better when you've rested."

I smiled limply. "I will."

"And for humanity's sake, Adam, don't stay up all night playing."

Adam looked at her earnestly. "Okay."

"You better not." Her brows snapped together. "If you're going to stay up late, it better be to improve your grades."

Adam's nose crinkled. "Yes, Ma."

Natalie wished us a goodnight and left me standing by the door, shuffling my feet unsure of what to do. I'd known there was a high chance I would spend the night in his room, and a part of me had been eager. I was curious to know how he was doing— I should have stalked his social media instead.

Adam huffed. "You know she likes you more."

I snorted and fell on Izzy's bed. "That's, like, impossible."

"I'm serious. She's always talking about Rasheed this and how great you're doing in school."

She had to be sorry for me. I had an absent mom, an overworked grandmother, and the rest of my family was an ocean away. Adam was unaware—about the absent mom at least. I'd always advertised Frida as a badass to save face. That she was the coolest person ever, jumping from country, capturing stories of people doing amazing things. I had even believed it.

I sprang up. "I'll go take that shower." I was not in the mood to reminisce about my life. "You got clothes I can borrow?"

*

Showers should be registered as a form of therapy; the exhaustion of the day fell away soon as the drops of water landed on my skin. The problem was the quietness of it gave me too much time to replay the day's events. Those five minutes between me stepping outside, eyeing the garden, and then Granma's fall. I wondered if there was something I could have done differently. Those five minutes had tilted the plane of my life.

Today made it hard to ignore I only had Granma in my corner. If she...*left* it would be Frida and me. Dear God, that sounded like a disaster waiting to happen. To explain our relationship, one would have to imagine an empty canvas, and I had been waiting a good chunk of my childhood for us to paint it together. But she'd never been there. Relying on her as a parent would be equivalent to giving a thirsty person an empty glass.

I tilted my head upward and let the water pummel my face, careful to keep it from entering my nose.

Anyway, Granma would heal, Frida would come and go, and life would go back to normal.

I got back to the room and burrowed under the heavy covers, facing the wall to avoid the screen's glare, and tried to sleep.

Chapter Five

My sleep was broken. I'd see myself in the hospital, holding Granma's hand, then Adam's chair would squeak or he'd jab at something, and I'd be jolted back to consciousness only for the cycle to repeat. I ended up in a coffin, lying next to Granma, who lay stiff as a statue next to me. I banged on the coffin trying to get it to open, but it would not. I started to panic at the sight of Granma: loose decaying skin, sunken eyes, blackened teeth. She made low growly noises, the same ones zombies made, and I knew for sure I had to jump ship, dream or not.

I jerked awake.

It was dark and quiet, and I was sleek with sweat. The unfamiliarity of the room made my panic swell. Was I still dreaming? Something rustled. I whipped my head in the direction of the sound. Adam. The tension released, and I relaxed. I was at the Herman house. No zombies here. I hated zombies. Hated them.

I fell back on the bed and stared at nothing as I tried to orient myself.

The universe had to be telling me something; maybe something had happened to Granma. I reached out a shaking hand for my phone on the nightstand and knocked something over. It landed on the thin rug with a heavy thud. Granma lying helpless on the floor flashed in my mind.

On the other side of the room, Adam sat up.

"It's me. Sorry, I knocked something over."

"Rasheed?" he said in a gravelly voice.

"Yeah."

My phone said it was only a few minutes past one. Paul was probably asleep, but that was irrelevant. I dialed his number; I had to know for sure if Granma was alright.

I should have stayed at the hospital.

The phone rang close to a minute before he picked up. "Rasheed? Something the matter?"

Forget about me. "How's Granma? Can I talk to her?"

"She's currently asleep. I don't want to wake her; she's not resting enough because they have to look at her every now and then. The doctor was here less than an hour ago to check on her, and he mentioned her vitals were okay."

I sighed. She was alive and breathing. I fell back on the bed and rubbed my chest.

"How are you doing?"

"I...I panicked—I thought..." I pinched the bridge of my nose. "I had a bad dream."

"She's doing well," Paul assured me, and maybe I was imagining it, but there was a smile in his voice.

"Okay."

A beat of silence. "If something happens, I'll call you, but nothing will."

"Thanks, Paul."

"Not a problem. Try and sleep."

I hummed even though I was sure that was not gonna happen. The exhaustion of the day had drained away, and my mind had become a buzz of activity. I made the promise anyway, apologized for waking him up, wished him a goodnight, and disconnected the call.

"What's up?" Adam asked.

"Making sure my dream was nothing more than that."

"Oh, so she's fine."

"Paul says so." And Paul didn't have a reason to lie.

"Who's Paul?"

"A friend...I guess." Though the evidence suggested there was more to it than friendship. I yawned.

"Want me to fire up the PC, give you something else to think about?"

"I'll pass. I still don't like video games."

"What do you do for fun?" He sounded scandalized.

I snorted. "I don't know—YouTube?" Adam mock gasped. "Look, we all don't have to like the same thing."

"I know." Sheets rustled. "Though I remember you being shit at them."

That was because he'd sit so close, his thigh pressed to mine, his body angled toward mine, making my mind lose focus as my brain turned all its attention to enhancing my skin's sensors so I could savor the moment. "Pretty sure I'm worse now."

There was a stretch of silence. "So, umm, when's Rukia leaving the hospital?"

"Monday."

Adam cleared his throat. "If you, uh, want to talk...I can listen. Don't promise to, you know, have answers, but I can listen if you want."

"That's...nice."

Adam and I had disliked each other the moment we met. To me, he was a pampered spoiled ass, and he got irritated at having to split Natalie's attention with one more person. We still hung out, though, because Granma worked long shifts at a nursing home, and Natalie wanted Adam to have a friend since he had none. If Peep hadn't become part of our "friendship," we'd have found a way to kill each other.

Instead, the dumbest thing happened—I got a crush on Adam.

Adam and I never discussed any emotional stuff. That was Peep's role. It was bad enough Adam had been put in charge of me—the kid from Africa with no English proficiency and a "weird" accent—to keep the bullies away. I didn't want him to see me as any more vulnerable. I thought it would turn him off. In the end, it hadn't mattered.

"Don't sound so surprised. Even villains take breaks and do mundane things like offer an ear," he said in what we once referred to as the butler accent.

I smiled. "Oh my God, the accent is still bad."

"Hold up—bad? You used to like them."

"I did?" I'd been hopelessly infatuated, and it had been horrific—Adam drinking water used to excite; my judgment back then had been compromised. The turn from seeing Adam as insufferable to Adam looking my way and making me trip over my own feet had given me whiplash.

"You were hyping me up for nothing?"

"You did nail the 'I need a bottle of water.' That was nice."

"That's, like, one line, and anyone can do it. I used to do that monologue about dreary weather and wearing coats and carrying an umbrella. I feel like a fool," he mumbled.

Bet you didn't fall for one of your best friends and then have said best friend send you mixed signals, then think for sure there could be something, only for them to fall in love with a girl with a cute button nose, then distance yourself thinking *that* would make them see they liked you, only for them to not notice. There had been crying too. Cue clown music.

The memories always made me wince and my chest pinch. Adam should have noticed we weren't spending as much time together because we were *friends* before I started fixating on his lips, but he never did, or he did and did not care. I doubted the validity of our friendship. Had that been in my mind? Were we really friends, or was he sticking around me because of his mom? Since we'd never reconnected, I figured it was the latter. And that made the pain even worse because on top of everything, I'd lost a friend too.

"Hey, you sleeping?"

I settled on my back and laid my head on my clasped hands. "Nope. Doubt I'll be getting sleep any time soon."

There was a stretch of silence. "Okay, uh, what have you been up to?"

"Nothing much. You?"

"Same."

That was such a lie. Adam had broken up with Sarah—the girl with the cute button nose—and people had talked about it *a lot*. All the cute couple pictures on both their social media accounts had been deleted or archived. Three years' worth of photos gone overnight. People had talked and speculated, but no one knew the real reason. Some said Sarah broke up with him by text because Adam forgot their anniversary. There was a wild one where Sarah had gotten pregnant, had an abortion, moved away at the beginning of the year, and eventually broke up with him. A part of me had wanted to reach out to Adam, but it hadn't been the right time.

The embarrassing part was realizing I'd been an avid follower of their relationship and could trace almost every important point in it.

Adam said something.

"What?"

He chuckled. "I've been speaking for a minute."

"Shit. Sorry, I got distracted."

"I get it," Adam said. "My offer still stands, you know."

"Yeah, I know."

"Come on." Adam jumped off the bed. "I know a place."

I sat up. Adam turned on a lamp. I squinted my eyes to keep the light from blinding me. "What?"

"A place, it's nice." Adam slipped on his sneakers.

I stared at him. "Last time you said that, I nearly got injured."

Adam's neighbors two doors down had turned their backyard into a winter wonderland—fake snow, fairy lights, balloon lamps. Adam wanted to show us but had conveniently forgotten to mention the big brown dog with a vicious bark. It was a good thing the frothing bastard had a leash, or I would have lost a leg.

Adam smiled. "Nothing extreme."

I gave him side-eye. "No dog?"

"We won't even be trespassing," Adam assured me.

"This better be nice." I kicked off the covers.

*

We made our way down the stairs with light steps, afraid to wake anyone, through the kitchen, the sliding doors, and out into the backyard. I stood admiring the pool that had been my third favorite thing about coming over—the second being Natalie.

"Rasheed!" Adam hissed. "Come on."

I followed.

The cobbled steps—I knew where they led. Past the small tree enclave was the playhouse. I squinted; it was still there, painted a bright pink color. We used it only when we were up to no good, or when Adam was angry with his family, or when he wanted privacy to make out with Sarah. "The playhouse?"

"Yeah."

"Aren't we a little too old?"

"Speak for yourself, grandpa. I still can't vote."

I grinned. "Fuck you very much."

Inside, the playhouse was dark and smelled like lemon air freshener and something else. I sniffed. "You brought me here for weed?"

"Yeah. But you don't have to smoke if you don't want to." Adam fiddled about before tea lights came on, illuminating the small space. The walls were neon-pink, covered in large flowers, each petal with a different pattern and color, and posters of pop icons, as well as dozens of a—I squinted my eyes—girl with the devil's smirk and glowing hands. The thin mattress on the floor added to the colorful chaos, with blue and orange throws and brightly patterned pillows. "What do you think?"

"Hmm. It's colorful?"

"Yeah, let's say Em and Maya are very imaginative." He fell back on the mattress and stretched out, his feet coming right to where I knelt.

"Who's the girl?" I pointed to one poster where the girl was grinning manically in a Superman pose.

"Some character on Disney, or Netflix. Not sure. She fights monsters or something. "You going to stay there?"

I crawled and lay on my back, bending my knees to fit my legs, and stared at the ceiling, which was painted black with glowing stars stuck to it. "She looks like a monster."

"I think she is—a reformed monster."

"Please don't tell me you invited me here to look at her all night?"

He chuckled, dug into his pocket, and produced a blunt and a lighter. "So I stole this from Izzy if you want. I was saving it for something, but I didn't know what. Or we can look at the creepy girl."

"I am not looking at the creepy girl."

Adam took the first inhale, exhaled, and handed it to me. I took a large inhale, sputtered a few times because it had been a while, and then blew out the smoke. If only my problems were the smoke particles, leaving me and dissolving into the air. I could only wish.

"So what have you really been up to?" Adam asked. "For the last four years."

"Hmm, let's see...there's school. I dated a couple of times; we broke up. Oh, I met Robert Downey, Jr."

"Holy shit!" Adam turned on his side so he could face me. "You're joking!"

"I am."

"You're an ass."

I laughed. "Sorry. To be fair, we met this guy, his name was Noel, and he looked exactly like him—the height, the goatee, everything. He let us get a picture with him. Want to see?"

"Sure."

I pulled out my phone, swiped a few times until I found the picture. I passed the phone to Adam. He took it, stared at it before he turned to me and then back at the screen. "Okay, they do look alike."

He handed the phone back. I flipped through the pictures before I pocketed the phone. "What about you? What have you been up to?"

"I had a mostly shitty year."

"Sorry about Sarah."

Adam shrugged and reached out his hand to pass the blunt. "It's what it is. On the upside, I made a new friend, Eric, who introduced me to coding, which kept my mind off everything."

"That's cool. Like, I don't know why when someone says they code, my mind goes to genius."

Adam waved at himself. "I won't argue with that."

I snorted.

"But you're not so bad. Mom says you're an honors student."

"Okay, I'm gonna spill the secret," I said. "Spend hours upon hours studying till my brain is fried. I was kind of jealous of you—you know, because of how fast you were able to understand shit. Remember you used to beat me at math, and I was *good* at math. I'm sure if you spent as many hours as I did studying, you'd probably...I don't know, find the solution to end world hunger?"

"Don't remind me. I'm bad at math now, like bad."

"What? Really?"

"Shocked you haven't heard my mom complain about it to your grandma."

"But you're smart."

"My grades beg to differ. So are you going to be a doctor?"

"God no. Remember Peep broke his arm and I couldn't stop vomiting? I'll be a business major and probably end up in marketing." Granma's disappointment had been palpable when I told her this. "But mostly, if I could make a choice, it would be to sleep and sunbathe all day."

"I tried to tell my dad that, and I got a whole speech about applying myself."

"Have you decided what you'll do after?"

"Not yet. I keep going back and forth between something to do with science, and modeling. Even becoming a monk sounds exciting."

I chortled with laughter.

"I can see you modeling but—"

"Are you saying I'm hot?"

There was a smile in his voice. I glanced at him; his lips were stretched wide, teeth gleaming. The dim lights played on his skin, making it look like polished copper.

"You must be high; I did not say that."

Adam laughed. "You so did, indirectly."

I ignored him. He did not need me inflating his head. "But a monk? You?"

"Okay maybe that won't work. Maybe I'll join a hippie commune. I'm all about that free-spirit stuff now, and not getting attached..." He was silent for a beat. "You ever get your heart broken?"

"Yes." By you. "It sucks."

He sighed. "Yeah, it does. It felt like a part of me was being cut out, every day."

"You two were together a long time."

Adam nodded. "Yeah, a long time and then..."

I shifted closer to him, put my hand on his and squeezed.

He huffed. "I keep thinking I'm over it, but I get pulled back every time."

"It'll dull enough you won't remember it, and one day the pain won't be so bad."

I thought of Scott. He had to have gone through shit after I ended our relationship. He'd said he loved me—first person to ever say it to me, and my brain had decided the most logical thing to do was to run away. My brain had failed to process "love," put up a large red flag, and completely dissociated.

"Probably." Adam grabbed my wrist. I expected him to push my arm away, but instead, he turned my hand and clasped it in his.

My brain went on high alert.

"This okay with you?" he asked.

"Umm, yes."

He tugged me closer. My gaze flicked to those lips. The lower one, a dull pink, appeared soft and—to my excitement—wet and open. He leaned in close. I parted my lips in anticipation, and he...he took a sniff of me.

"You still smell the same," he said in a breathy whisper. "Your grandma still burns incense?"

I slumped. "Yes, Granma still believes it keeps *jinis* away." She didn't like the idea of evil spirits roaming our house with confidence.

I untangled our fingers with the pretense of scratching my thigh and made sure the rest of the evening we maintained some personal space.

Chapter Six

Identical faces hovered over me.

I tightened my grip on the covers as I prepared for fight mode. One of the faces morphed into a wide grin, cheeks dimpling. I blinked, tried to clear the sleep and orient myself to my surroundings. Twins. Em and Maya, who were nothing like the short, sticky five-year-olds with a mountain of nagging questions I'd known.

My mouth was dry, tongue stuck to the roof. I needed food and water—a truckload of both. "Umm, hey. You're grown and stuff."

One twin rolled her eyes. "It's what kids do."

They skipped to the other end of the room and started to poke and prod Adam. "Come on. Dad said you had to watch over us." They had thick towels wrapped around them, one purple and the other blue, and wore matching bright-pink caps and yellow flip-flops.

"Give me five minutes." Adam grumbled. "I swear Ma should have dragged you to church."

"Three minutes."

"We'll be back."

They skipped out of the room, and I reached for my phone. Paul had sent texts. I held my breath. *Hey Eedy, it's me. I'm about to go into surgery. I'll see you when I'm done.* The second text asked me to bring some personal stuff. I exhaled in relief.

Adam made growling noises, then kicked off the bedsheets and rolled out of bed, onto the floor. "Another day of wishing I was an only child."

I lay flat on my stomach and looked at him over the edge of the bed. His shirtless state showed off a defined body, suggesting he did regular exercise. I stared a long time, fascinated with the way his torso curved and dipped. "You'd hate it."

"Maybe." He pulled himself up, grabbed the sheets, and threw them on the bed. "Come on; let's go before they come back. I need food."

We got ourselves downstairs, and the twins vibrated with excitement as they rushed toward the pool. Large and rectangular, its aqua-blue color reminded me of the ocean. The beach had been my first love back in Mombasa, where it had been a short ride away. I'd tried to go there every Saturday if Granma let me.

Adam had me watch them as he went to get breakfast. They took turns on the springboard, doing jumps and splashing as much water as they could.

"Here we are." Adam handed me one of the plates in his hands, piled with store-bought waffles. He turned to the twins. "You guys ate, right?"

"Yeah, we ate."

Adam left and came back with glassfuls of orange juice and settled next to me on the lounge chair, thankfully leaving inches of space between us.

"I thought they'd be swimming," I said, nodding at the twins.

The one in the red swimsuit—Maya? Emily?—called out, "This is more fun."

"There was a clip of twin boys doing synchronized diving going around, and now they want to be like them; that means I have to give up an hour or two of my life because I have to watch them." Adam pouted. It was cute.

"That's right, or we tell Ma about all the sneaking out you do."

"And they're blackmailers too."

"Sounds a lot like you at that age."

Adam shook his head. "Absolutely false."

"Oh yeah? Remember when you had me do your homework after I accidentally broke a vase."

Adam laughed. "Dude, I had to capitalize on your fear, but you had to know my mom wouldn't have done anything to you."

"That's not how you told it, you ass. You made it sound like she'd kill me." I'd been afraid Natalie wouldn't want me around anymore if I was a nuisance. "I hope you guys get money from him too."

Their cheeks dimpled. "We do."

"Don't encourage them."

"And we know about last night."

I flushed with heat. "Huh?"

"Told you not to encourage them."

"Yup." The girl in the blue one-piece walked to the edge of the springboard. "But watch this—I think I finally have it down."

She got into position to do a headfirst dive and plunged in. I winced at her landing. A slight change in the angle and her fall would have probably ended in injury.

"Not bad," Adam said to the twin before turning to me. "Didn't you used to be a pro swimmer?"

"What—no?" I'd been an enthusiastic swimmer with potential if I'd gotten the right guidance. But the swim team had a bigot for a coach; he killed the whole vibe. He was nothing like Lowela—a lifeguard at Nyali beach. She'd been patient and kind while tutoring me. "But I have some tips I can share with you."

The twins grinned. "Awesome."

Looking at their excited faces reminded me of my own eagerness when Lowela had started teaching me by explaining the nature of water and the ocean first, how vast and beautiful it was, but also how dangerous it could be. Most of the words went over my head as I was too impatient to get started.

I explained to the twins about the best form for the headfirst dive, how to position their hands and legs to avoid any injury. Adam helped explain in a way they could understand, and soon enough, they were attempting the dive with a little more finesse. Em, in red, managed to do a half-decent dive and shrieked in delight.

"You should teach us," Maya said.

"Umm..."

"You would, right?" Emily beamed.

"Rasheed is nice; he'd never say no to that."

I glared at Adam. "We'll see." Sure, by Wednesday, they'll have moved on to other interests—if they were anything like Adam.

Mr. Herman showed up. He had a two-inch well-combed Afro with streaks of gray, and was broad-shouldered, with light skin and a pointed jaw. He wore a suit and tie that made him look intimidating.

Adam straightened on his seat as Mr. Herman scanned us with brown-hazel eyes like watered-down mud. "Rasheed is it?"

"Yes, sir."

Adam rolled his eyes. Mr. Herman, in his suit and that locked jaw, screamed *I'm in charge.* I remembered he'd been head of a department before he started his own consulting firm.

He expressed concern for Granma and asked me about school, and I answered the way I would a college interviewer. Mr. Herman, seeming pleased with my answers, nodded. "That's good, really good."

"Dad, I'm taking Rasheed to the hospital, so I won't be in."

My eyebrows went up. He was? "Thanks, but you don't really have to."

"I'd like to; it's been a while since I saw your Granma."

"Cool. She'll like that," I said.

And if the idea of spending more time with him made my mind fuzzy with excitement, that was no one's business.

Chapter Seven

We found Granma resting in bed with Paul by her side. Seeing he wore the same clothes from yesterday instilled a sense of camaraderie toward him. I was not in this alone.

"This is Paul." I pointed to Paul, unsure of how to introduce him. Friend was an understatement. "This is Adam, Natalie's son."

"Nice to meet you," Paul said.

"Adam! Nice of you to come visit," Granma said. "I haven't seen you in forever."

He rubbed the back of his neck. "Sorry about that. Been busy with school."

"How was it?" I asked Granma.

"It was a success."

Peep, Mo, and Tani's voices filtered into the room from the hallway. They were arguing about the direction to Granma's room.

Peep stepped into the room first, wearing his usual head-to-toe black. His arm was linked with Tani's. Mo trailed them looking like an Instagram model in faded blue jeans and a shirt with doodles on it. Peep did a double take at Adam's presence and greeted him with enthusiasm, like a long-lost friend, even though I was sure they had a couple of classes together.

Granma huffed. "Can't believe the most visitors I get are teenagers."

"I brought something," Tani said, untangling from Peep to reach into her sling bag.

"Tani, I am not dying."

Tani shrugged and handed her the wrapped gift. "I know; still, I love giving out gifts."

"You didn't get me a gift for my birthday," Mo pointed out.

"I signed the card 'Peep and Tani,' didn't I?" Peep said.

"You call a card a gift?" Mo spat, his eyebrows pulled together.

"You gave me a pen," I pointed out.

"You like pens."

"It was a chewed-on pen."

Beside me, Adam cackled.

Granma tore open the wrapping paper and found a colorful notebook inside.

"To take notes in of things you like from the books you read," Tani explained.

"The *one* book she reads," I muttered under my breath.

"What's that?" Granma squinted her eyes at me.

I smiled brightly. "Nothing."

"You never finish reading a book, Rukia," Paul teased.

Granma shook her head. "That's a lie."

"Haven't you and Ma been reading, like, one book since the year started?" Adam asked.

"Sometimes you don't even reach midway," I added.

Granma huffed. "I don't like being ganged up on. I have a heart condition."

"You can use it to outline your novel."

Granma smiled and hugged the notebook. "I like that idea." She studied the notebook. "I think I have an idea already. Tell me what you think—an old woman is reaching for something from a top shelf, falls, knocks her head on a hard surface and is taken back to her twenties and given the chance to do life again. The book ends with the woman in a coma and all that was in her head. When she wakes up, she's injured a part of her brain and thinks she's still in her twenties."

"That's like some dark episode from *Black Mirror*," Peep commented.

"They're all dark," Adam said.

I frowned. Was she referring to her life?

"I'd absolutely read it," Mo volunteered. "I like weird stuff like that, and maybe there should be a sequel where it turns out some evil witch locked the part of her brain that is tied to the present to stop her from ruining the witch's evil plan."

Tani scrunched her face. "What? How even?"

Granma considered it. "Let's even go ahead and say the witch is her twin sister, so we can say they have the same brain wavelength. Anyone with a pen?"

"And even say the witch had been frozen, and the good twin falling woke her up because of the connection. So it's like the witch is using her twin's power to stay awake," Adam put in.

I slightly elbowed him. "Granma, no. That's a horrible idea."

But Granma was already writing it down with the pen Paul had handed her, and Peep joined in with even more outrageous ideas. Paul, too, and then Tani and me, against our wills, were pulled in on it. That was how we passed the next few hours, managing to fill about ten pages with absurd ideas.

Granma flipped through the pages, and I saw the questioning look in her eye. Even though the ideas were honestly horrific, I hoped she could get halfway this time.

Peep cleared his voice to catch our attention. "I got to get home."

"Oh my, it's late," Granma said, putting the notebook on the side table. "Thank you for coming Peep. You, too, Mo, and thank you Tani for the book."

"We couldn't *not* come," Mo said, and Granma sighed.

"Good luck with the book," Tani added.

I walked them out.

In the parking lot, Adam waved goodbye and got into his car. The goodbye was inadequate; there should have been more—a hug, a lingering look. Something. This felt too final. It probably was, but maybe things would change. Maybe when we saw each other in the hallways, we would nod at each other in acknowledgement.

Peep nudged me with his elbow. "Did the cold war end?"

I shrugged. "I don't know."

I headed back to Granma's room after we exchanged our goodbyes, Peep's question playing in my mind. God, I hoped the stalemate was over because I would have liked it if Adam and I were friends again.

Chapter Eight

Paul drove me home and, like me, was too tired to bother with a conversation.

The mingled scents of vanilla, coconut, and incense met me at the door. Being home was not as satisfying as I had imagined because of the odd silence. I cleaned up, threw the dough in the trash, and cleared the counter and sink.

Soon as I fell into bed, I dozed off.

The next morning, the smell of burnt toast hung to the air. I scrunched my nose, confused. Granma was supposed to be in the hospital unless all that had been a very detailed dream—for which I'd be eternally grateful and probably sacrifice a goat or two in gratitude.

I rushed to the kitchen.

It was Frida. Frida was here, at home, standing in the kitchen making toast. I blinked. She wore a white shirt with brown khakis. She turned before I had time to compose myself. Her eyes widened. "Rasheed!" She fumbled with the glass in her hand, spilling some water.

"Hi."

"You're...tall."

Yup, courtesy of you mother dearest. Frida was half a head shorter than me. Unless my father, who I'd never known or seen, had indeed been a giant. Our height was the only indicator we were related. The universe's way of maintaining balance. Not that she was ugly— She had high, cutting cheek bones and an oval face, a slender neck and lovely almond eyes. I didn't think I would have been okay seeing her in me every time I was in front of the mirror.

"I've been drinking lots of milk." I hovered, unsure of what to do.

Frida blinked and gestured to the kettle. "There's tea and toast, if you want?"

I stepped into the kitchen and reached for a mug. "When'd you get here?"

"Around three." She put down the glass and glanced at me.

Silence fell.

"I want to rest a little before I go see Mama."

"Sounds good."

She grabbed a slice of toast and started out of the kitchen. She paused at the threshold and turned to me. "It's good to see you."

"Oh."

Frida nodded in a way that said "nice talk" before she headed toward her room. It stayed empty all year except for the extensive collection of documentaries and gigantic encyclopedias. As a kid, I was in there most evenings, creating scenarios in my head of us doing stuff together.

I cocked my head and waited to see her usual march. Because Frida either marched or crept—walking was not for her. How was Rukia Frida's mom? Rukia, who moved as if she had the world in her palm, as if the world was waiting for her.

Except this time, Frida *walked*. Her steps were more fluid than I'd ever seen, and the stiffness, though there, was not as prominent.

As soon as I got back to my room, I texted the guys: *Okay, aliens came while we were sleeping.*

PEEP: *you don't believe in aliens.*

ME: *I'm rethinking it*

MO: *you're tired, drink coffee.*

MO: *is this about your mom?*

ME: *kind of*

PEEP: *she came? What'd she do?*

ME: *she did...she walked like a human, not stiff and got a stick up her ass...*

MO: *aha...*

ME: *that's it*

Mo sent a GIF of someone smacking their face.

PEEP: *are you high?*

I sent back middle fingers.

PEEP: *anyway, follow the link attached to read Tani's latest poem.*

MO: *bro, that stuff is so cringe*

PEEP: *and you wonder why you got a card for your birthday*

I threw the phone on the bed; this was something.

Chapter Nine

I couldn't stop yawning later that day. The adrenaline rush from the weekend was starting to wear down, and I found myself dozing during most of my classes, much to Miss Havan's disgust. But she had this soft, droning sound that made you want to reach for a pillow and a blanket.

Frida's alto and Granma's melodic voice greeted me in the doorway. I kicked off my shoes and rushed to the kitchen as a new surge of energy rushed through me. Granma sat at the dining table, which was only a stretch of the arm from the kitchen, and Frida was chopping vegetables. Relief and joy at having Granma home and healthy washed over me like a cool breeze on a sunny day. I mumbled a greeting; Frida managed a small smile and a glance in my general direction before she went back to chopping.

"*Usikate* carrot *ziwe kubwa hivyo*," Granma said.

The carrots in question were large enough to choke a baby, and nothing got Granma off food faster than Hulk-sized carrot pieces.

Frida replied in Swahili, "They're not even that big."

Ravenous, I rummaged through the fridge in hopes of finding a snack—leftover pizza or even a molding slice of bread. To my disappointment, there were only leafy greens and fruits, our leftovers gone. I blew out air in frustration. This was Frida's handiwork. She seemed allergic to snacks and junk food; another sign she most likely was not as human as she presented.

"What are you cooking?" I asked in Swahili and cringed at how bad my accent had gotten. I'd decided on losing it after this kid had broken into peals of laughter when he heard me call Granma *nyanya*, the Swahili word for grandmother. Looking back, I should never have let a kid with elephant ears send me into an identity crisis. The accent had gone but, it seems, also my competence in Swahili.

"*Wali wa nazi na urojo.*"

"Don't forget to put the cinnamon stick," Granma instructed.

"Yes, you mentioned it."

"Shouldn't you be resting?" I asked.

"I've had enough sitting and doing nothing."

"Because you were sick," Frida pointed out. She side-eyed Granma. The resemblance was uncanny, same high cheekbones, same wide dark eyes, and same oval face.

"No one is keeping me out of my kitchen."

"Because you think I can't prepare rice and the *urojo*." Frida gathered the carrots and threw them in the pan. The pan sizzled, and the smell of the spices rose up; my stomach rumbled.

"I know you can, but I need to make sure."

Frida shut her eyes and pinched her lips.

I reached for a box of cereal, poured some in a bowl and added milk, then headed to my room. The distance from the kitchen to my bedroom door could be covered in a few large steps. I threw my backpack on the desk by the door and flopped onto the bed, wedged in one corner of the room by the window.

I gobbled down the cereal. Satisfied at having my stomach full, I was now in a horizontal position, and Granma was home and well.

"Peace at last," I murmured to myself. A sizable amount of homework waited for me, a test on Friday, a full week of school ahead, which meant more dodging—absolutely beside the point.

To avoid fixating on the bad, I picked up my phone and started cruising through Instagram. Mo had posted a picture of a thick manga with the caption: enjoying this. I snorted. Dude thought he was being slick, as if anyone could miss the soft hands at the edge of the photo, one wrist covered in a pink gold bracelet, and her left middle finger with a silver ring curved into a spider. He was referring to Malia. I left a Like, ignored the urge to send a text messing with him, and continued scrolling. Further down, I came across Izzy's post, a picture of him shirtless with a heavy weight on his shoulders proving he was not the lamppost everyone mistook him for. Adam was the first to comment with a thumbs-up emoji.

Adam's latest post made my eyes bug and heat pool in my stomach, and a little lower. Oh, wow. A short video showed Adam bench pressing, shirtless, in biker shorts. The way his muscles pulled together and then expanded made me dizzy with excitement.

He looked like a snack.

Or all my favorite snacks rolled into one.

I hit Like, then watched it a dozen more times. My eyes latched on to a drop of sweat trickling down the side of his face before God finally granted me the strength to turn off my phone, haul myself to my desk, and open my chemistry books. I found the right page and stared at it. Atoms. My eyes glazed as images of muscles and smooth, dark-brown skin fogged my mind. Focus, Rasheed... I shook my head. Atoms. Focus on atoms.

Frida knocked on my door a while later and announced the food was ready.

I loaded my plate and carried it to the living room where Granma was watching a hospital drama with this guy who had a jaw that could cut through steel, so of course I sat my ass down to watch.

I did a double take. Paul was seated in Granma's floral armchair, the only furniture in the living room that wasn't from garage sales or thrift stores. "Oh, hey Paul." I slid in next to Granma on the couch, directly facing the television.

"Hello," he answered.

Frida joined us and sat in the armchair Granma was always threatening to throw away. She sank nearly to the floor with a shriek, legs off the ground, but acted fast enough to stop her plate from spilling. The awkward angle made her look comical; I sucked in my lower lip to stop from laughing.

"So sorry about that." Granma said. "I'm always saying I'll throw it out."

"You should." Frida managed two tries before she got her feet under her. I shoved the rice in my mouth.

"Come sit with us."

Frida looked from me to Granma and the space between us. "It's fine." She pushed the cushion around and found the right angle to let it hold her weight, then sat down gingerly.

"I will fix it for you as soon as I can," Paul said.

"Thank you." They exchanged smiles that had Granma's cheeks perking up.

My eyebrows furrowed. This again? "I think it's time you let it go," I muttered.

"This is great, Frida." Paul pointed with his spoon to the mountain of food on his plate. "Really nice."

"Thank you, Paul," Frida said quietly. She turned to Granma with a triumphant look. Granma ignored her.

"A little more black pepper wouldn't have hurt."

Frida sighed.

"Oh, I forgot to tell you I saw someone with a folding phone." Paul turned to me.

While Paul had been fixing loose floorboards, he'd started up an awkward conversation I would have preferred to abandon, but Granma had tattooed the "respect your elders" philosophy into my bones, and I couldn't escape it. The conversation had turned out to be interesting once Paul and I found we both had a love for mobile technology. "Really?"

"Yeah, I am really tempted to get one."

"Wow," Granma said and chuckled. "To think a few years back, I used to queue up to use *zile simu za* Telkom, remember Frida? And those first few years after you left Mombasa, we didn't talk for months?"

Not like there was much communication now, I thought.

"Yeah, I do."

"Made international calls a pain," Paul said. "I think I went several years without hearing from most of my family after I moved here."

They launched into talk of migration and culture shock and life back in Kenya—Granma missing her friends in Mombasa, and Paul missing his family in Kisumu. I had learned never to bring up the weather when they were both in the same room. I shushed them. Granma glared at me. I grinned apologetically.

*

Granma cleared her throat and then did it again. We turned to her. Satisfied she had our attention, she said, "I want to share some good news." My mind was on her getting a raise or maybe—and this is would have been the preferred option—getting rid of her dying Honda.

"*Mi na Paul tumeamua kufunga ndoa.*"

My brain caught the words but failed to compute the meaning behind them. My Swahili was rusty, and I had reached the point where the best I could manage was greetings and basic one-liners, and a slow processing speed of the uncommon words. I was a step away from *hakuna matata* bad. I turned the words slowly over in my mind. *Mi na Paul tumeamua kufunga ndoa.* I broke the words down: *Mi na Paul*—Paul and I, *tumeamua*—we have agreed, *kufunga ndoa*—to get married.

Paul and I have agreed to get married.

I choked on my rice. I placed the bowl on the table to avoid dropping it—on the recently vacuumed carpet and incurring Granma's wrath—and started hacking, pounding on my chest to get the rice down my windpipe.

Granma patted my back two times, more to soothe than anything. "It's not that big of an issue; it seemed right. Right, Paul?"

"Yes, absolutely right."

I wheezed, clawing at my throat. My face started to get hot, my throat itched, and my eyes started to water.

"Mama, I think he's chocking," Frida said.

Paul, bless him, quickly jumped up pulled me from the seat, turned me around, and started performing the Heimlich maneuver. After three pumps, the rice dislodged from my throat. Paul released me, and I fell on the couch, my eyes wet and snot running down my nose.

Granma patted me up and down with a critical eye.

"Water," I rasped.

"Frida, *nenda kamletee glasi ya maji.*"

As Frida went to fetch me a glass of water, Granma pulled me into a tight hug and squished my face against her boobs.

"You'll suffocate me," I wheezed, throat rough as sand paper.

"*Pole.* Sorry" She let go and turned to rubbing my back. "Paul, you saved his life. Thank you."

Frida handed me a glass of water. I met her eyes, hoping for a sliver of affection after I nearly died—entirely possible, by the way—but she averted her gaze. I ignored the pinch in my heart. I should be used to the lack of caring from her. I was eighteen; the pain should have lessened. I exhaled and drained the water in four large gulps.

Paul squeezed her shoulder before he took his seat. "When I was young, a friend of a friend choked on a fish bone and died. He was only twenty-four, and the tragic part was his mother sold fish for a living."

"Oh, that's horrible," Granma said. "Someone must have bewitched him, then."

"Are you seriously getting married?" I squeaked.

Granma nodded and let her hand fall from my back. "Yeah, we are. Paul proposed to me while I was in the hospital, and I said yes."

Is that why Granma had wanted Paul to stay? Paul glanced at me expectantly. I dug my fingers into my thighs and fixed my eyes on the bowl of rice.

I waited for Frida to say something. I was her least priority, but I knew she'd go through Jupiter's hurricane for Granma—that was how we'd ended up in America. Shit had gone down, and Frida had done everything she could to ensure we immigrated here. But she only managed a "congratulations" and continued to sit stiffly, as if she'd been in the freezer for too long.

Was I being dramatic? Sure, they'd known each other for—what? A year now? A year was not long enough in my opinion—I'd settle for a decade.

OhmyGod!

The calls, the meals, Paul helping around... Had they been—dating? Right under my nose? Gross. My home was no longer sacred, not only was there an alien in our midst, but traitors too.

I stayed silent and focused on finishing my rice so could I retreat to my room as soon as possible to organize my thoughts. I threw myself on the bed, grabbed my phone, and brought up the group thread. I needed to vent.

ME: *GRANMA AND PAUL ARE GETTING MARRIED!!*

I tapped on the screen impatiently. Willing one of them to reply.

MO: *rotfl...for real???*

PEEP: *WHAT??*

ME: yup

MO: *lol...that's wild. Tell her congratulations.*

PEEP: *Good for her!*

ME: *stop laughing, Mo. And it's NOT a good thing.*

At all. Was I being delusional? No, I wasn't. I knew what I was talking about.

MO: *how's it a bad thing?*

Old memories rose from the darkest corners of my mind, drenched and heaving, they sank their teeth into my skin. Me scared and crying. Blood on the brown tiles. The crunch of bone breaking. Had Granma forgotten how her marriage to Babu Musa had ended?

Chapter Ten

"There goes your boy." Peep nodded behind me, and I froze, ready to bolt if it was Scott or duck and allow the crowded hallway to swallow me up. It was only Vick in plaid pants with an orange shirt, and as he got closer, I noticed the neon-green shoes he had on. I sighed in relief.

Peep burst out laughing. "You should have seen your face!"

I showed him my middle finger.

Mo succeeded in prying his gaze from the mirror glued to his locker; he'd been patting and prodding his high-top Afro fade to make sure no hair was out of place. "Why would anyone allow him to leave the house with neon-colored shoes matched with plaid?" Mo's face scrunched up like he'd bitten into a sour lemon.

"Guys, let's get back to me," I whined. Granma getting married was serious; the lack of reaction from Frida was unsettling.

"So your mom said nothing?" Peep asked.

"Frida," I corrected.

The word never suited her; even as a child, it had come off odd. Frida had won the Diversity Visa Lottery and left for America three months before I turned two years old. After that, I saw her a total of four times. I remembered begging her to take me with her. Granma had explained she was putting herself through school, but once she was done, she would take me with her. But even with the lack of distance between us, her schooling completed, she never made an effort to be a mom. A few months after we settled in Brooksville, she jumped on the first opportunity to leave for a video producer job in Atlanta before landing a good deal shooting business documentary series that took her around the globe.

"Absolutely nothing," I continued. "She went on as if Granma hadn't dropped a bombshell, congratulated her and stuff. I let it slide, thinking she's being polite and waiting until Paul left. But when he did leave, she cleared the kitchen and went to bed."

"What'd you want her to say?" Mo asked.

"Talk some sense into Granma!" Why were they not getting it? "I want to grab Granma's shoulders and shake some sense into her." Peep and Mo looked at me like I was speaking Swahili. "I'm just saying—they need more time to think this through."

"Maybe they did; there's tax benefits to being married," Peep said. "They're adults. Your Granma has raised two generations. And you said Paul has had about ten kids from three different women?"

"Three kids from three different women." Paul had apparently gotten carried away with sexual liberation—I really wish I had never heard that.

"Right. I'm sure they know what they're doing."

"Adults make mistakes all the time," Mo said. "I have an idiot older brother who's always losing his money in new ventures."

"Thank you," I said and patted Mo's shoulder.

"Your brother is a man-child; doesn't count," Peep said.

Out the corner of my eye, I noticed Adam. He was talking to a guy wearing a band shirt, with wild hair that covered part of his face. Adam laughed; his voice carried over the mass of people and settled on my skin like warm rays of sunshine. I wanted to know why he was laughing. I also wanted him to look my way. I remembered a time when Peep, Adam, Sarah, and I had gone to the movies— I'd worn my tightest shirt and even tighter jeans, light makeup, and shiny lip gloss, hoping Adam would notice me and dump Sarah. I winced. I had more sense now.

Peep elbowed me. "Is that the reason you're on this block?"

I straightened and pulled on my backpack straps, hitching it higher. "No, I'm going to see Mrs. Ballad."

"College essay?" Mo asked.

"Yes."

"I'm shocked y'all are not on a first-name basis yet."

*

As I headed to the bike rack after school, I saw Adam making his way through the parking lot as he thumbed his phone. I wanted to talk to him again—for the sake of friendship, not because of the way his thumb had rubbed over my hand or how his skin had glowed in the faint light.

"Hey Adam!" I called out.

He stopped walking and looked around. His eyes landed on me and widened in surprise. He started toward me, which was unexpected.

"Hey," I said. He was close enough to touch and that was really tempting.

"Hi." He beamed. "How's everything?"

Do not think about Granma on the floor; do not think about her on the floor. Do not think about Frida being alien. Don't think about Granma announcing she was getting married. "Not bad. You?"

"Same." He reached into his cloud of hair, picked at a lock, and twirled it between his fingers. *So this was not awkward.* He let go and straightened. "Listen, Maya has been on me to ask you to tutor her in swimming. That cool with you?"

I tried to picture which one was Maya. Both twins had the same styled box braids and same, well, everything. "Umm, I'm not sure."

I felt like an ass saying that. This should have been a sure thing. Growing up, Mrs. Herman would squeeze my shoulder and give me fond smiles the same way she would with Adam. The Hermans had been nothing but kind, and a part of me had wondered how I would repay that. Right here was the chance.

"It's cool," he said. "I told them you were probably busy, but that won't stop them from spamming your Instagram. They found it."

I shuffled my feet. "They're on Instagram?"

"A stan account; they're my biggest fans."

I laughed at that. "You really got a big head on you."

"I'm calling it as I see it; you did say I'd make a good model."

"I was high."

"It still counts." He shrugged. "If you change your mind you can always DM me?"

His attention on me caused heat to climb up my face. I rolled my eyes. "Going to make fun of me for liking your photo?"

Adam smiled. "Not making fun. I am reminding myself."

"I've liked your photos before."

"Not really."

"Yeah, I have."

"Trust me, you haven't."

"This is not a debate."

"'Cause you'll lose."

Then I spied the pink hair tips. Scott. He had a group of friends surrounding him, talking and laughing. Shit. He hadn't noticed me yet. I had enough time to get the hell out of there. "I gotta go, bye."

Adam brows furrowed. "Uh, bye."

"Sorry, talk later." I rushed to my bike, got on it, and booked it out of there.

I avoided turning back, even if I was itching to find out if Scott had seen me. Ignorance was bliss.

*

As I watered Mrs. Clay's garden, I made sure to put away any thoughts of Scott in an impenetrable safe. It had been two whole months since my cowardly exit from the relationship, and I was still haunted. Surely it should not have been that hard to say it. Even a "thanks" would have been marginally better than me skipping out on him.

Think other thoughts.

Think Adam, swimming, and twins.

The twins wanting me to tutor them gave me an ego boost. I wasn't that great of a swimmer or diver, but the idea did appeal to me.

One, I loved swimming. My earliest memories were of swimming in the Indian Ocean and the salty water burning my eyes because my dumbass-self opened them underwater. I would only get out when my skin was ashy and nearly white, then go in search of fried cassava, coaxing the hawker to put in as much *pilipili na ndimu* as he could. That was why my taste buds could only register too sweet or too spicy.

Two, the twins seemed decent. As decent as nine-year-olds could be anyway.

Three, an excuse to be out of the house would be nice.

The only problem was Adam. Dude was attractive, I was too aware, and that was a red flag. I couldn't go down that road again; last time it had ended badly.

Though that wasn't the only path; we could be platonic. We could be friends. Having a friend never hurt—okay, it did that once, but it didn't have to be a second time because this time, I had learned rationality.

Plus, texting him appealed to me—a way for us to get to know each other again, laying a foundation for a new *friendship*. I smiled at that, and my heart beat with excitement.

I sent Adam a message on my phone. *Will weekends work?*

I had a text from Peep. *Saw how quick you ducked out of the lot...LMFAO. For how long will you do that?*

I grumbled. Maybe forever? I groaned. I'd been here before with Adam. It'd been torturous. I had to find another way.

*

Frida was in the kitchen cleaning and organizing when I got home. It smelled like processed lemon and bleach, and I paused to take in the now polished and tidy countertops, the clean stovetop, and empty sink.

"Hey," I said.

"Hi."

I grabbed the bread and made a peanut butter sandwich; her eyes on me made me fumble with the butter knife. The silence that hung over us made my skin tingle with unease, nothing new. It was stupid to think something about her was different because her walk was less stiff.

I brushed it off. She would be gone in a few days.

My phone pinged as I retreated to my room, giving me something else to focus on.

ADAM: *Saturday Em has soccer. Sunday morning there's church, afternoon okay with you?*

ME: *yeah, that's fine*

ME: *they won't like try to lead me to demons or something?*

ADAM: *they'll try*

Chapter Eleven

A whole week after her arrival, instead of leaving, Frida had put the house in order and, to Granma's and my disgust, continued to stock the fridge with more vegetables and fruits. Granma was all about that *raha*—ease— insisting life was too short to hold herself back when it came to food.

I tried my best to ignore Frida's presence and the way she'd stiffen when we passed each other. I avoided ending up alone in the same room as her.

This was surprisingly easy as Granma was homebound, recovering from her surgery, and Paul was always over to attend to her, making her tea, ensuring she took her medicine on time, and questioning Frida on every food she prepared—if it was nutritious and good for her heart. All the while, no one brought up the wedding business, or Paul's constant presence, or how Frida was still around. Like, I was just meant to accept that this was life.

I daydreamed about it being Sunday already. I was eager for a day spent in water, away from home.

Sunday afternoon finally came, and I biked to the Herman house.

Adam opened the door wearing a vest that exposed his defined arms. He grinned. "Hey, come in." He stepped aside. "They've been waiting, asking every ten seconds if you're still coming."

The video of him bench pressing came to mind, very detailed and clear. I swallowed hard. All was still fine, no cause for alarm—no attraction would be happening. "Hey." I stepped inside. "I'm here now."

"Let me get them; meet you by the pool." He turned back and headed for the stairs, taking them two at a time, the loose basketball shorts framing his ass.

I shook my head.

The twins came down dressed in matching blue one-pieces and floral caps. I did a double take. They were very, umm, identical, almost as if they'd been made in a factory: oval faces, deep dimples, round eyes, same height, same round belly. Even their expressions mirrored each other. "Y'all are messing with me."

"It's the only one that was clean," said the one standing to my left with a dimpled grin.

Adam shook his head. "Really? Aren't you always insisting on individuality?"

"We are not—" Both of them started, then stopped and turned to glare at each other.

"We're different," one said.

"The other ones were dirty."

I turned to Adam pleadingly. What had I gotten myself into? Twins? Identical nine-year-old twins? This was bound to be a disaster.

Adam narrowed his eyes, flicking them between the two. He pointed to the one on the left. "This one's Maya." He pointed to the one on the right. "This one's Emily."

I nodded. "Okay." Left—Maya. Right—Emily. Now if only they would stay that way the rest of the time. "I think I have it." I studied them. How was it possible for them to look so much alike?

Adam saw my troubled expression and shifted closer. "If they're trouble...drown them," he whispered. I snorted.

"I heard that."

"Yeah, me too."

Adam turned to them and grinned wide. "I said crown them; you like being princesses, right?"

"You sound dumb," the one on the left said. Maya? No Emily.

"I'll see you guys later." Adam turned to leave. Alarmed, I reached for his hand, my fingers circling his forearm. It was firm and ridiculously smooth—so smooth I wanted to caress it.

I quickly let go and pocketed my hand. "You're leaving?"

"I'm going to save virtual princesses and kill some wraiths." He made a slashing motion.

"I've never been around kids on my own." I lowered my voice. "Like never. Last time I was around kids on my own, I was a kid."

"You guys will be good to Rasheed, right?"

A beat. "Does playing dead count?"

My eyes widened.

"Absolutely no on the playing dead." He slapped my arm and grinned. "They'll be good, and if they're not..." He brought his hands to his neck and pretended to choke, and then let his head loll to the side. I broke into laughter. He gave me a thumbs-up, and I followed the twins into the yard.

"Okay, how do we start this?"

I exhaled. I turned to the twins. Tried to figure out who'd spoken and gave up. Acting unsure was out of the question. Like predators, kids knew how to sniff out weakness. "With vigorous exercise," I said.

Both frowned, in harmony.

"That's a joke, right?"

"We'll start with stretches."

We did the stretches and started them off with the basics. I got on the springboard and demonstrated the best posture for diving. I stood arms high, toes curled around the edge of the board as a shiver of excitement skated over my skin. It had been too long since I'd swum—last summer had been spent selling blenders and moping around indoors trying to get over my breakup. I inhaled, held my breath and dived.

The water enveloped me, rushed against my ears and cancelled out all noise. This had fascinated me as a kid. Nyali Beach would get so noisy and crowded, especially in December, but once the water swallowed me, the world was drowned out, only the sound of blood rushing in my ear. Submerged in water, the troubles of the world muted; it felt safe.

I opened my eyes, expecting seaweed and legs planted in the sand, and the maddening burn of salt water in my eyes. Instead, there was only clear, crystal-blue and a slight pinch in my eyes caused by the chlorine. I shut them and started swimming. I tried to stay under as long as possible. My lungs started to burn. I brought my head up, inhaled, and continued kicking until I got to the other end of the pool.

"That was pretty cool," Maya said.

I bowed my head, grinning. "Thank you. Now let's see if you got it."

We went over my instructions from last Sunday, fixing their postures, improving their angles. I was decent at handling the kids. I mentally patted myself on the back. I had them try to dive one last time before I called an end to the session. Em got on the diving board first and shifted her body to mimic the correct posture. I gave her a thumbs-up while she got ready. She miscalculated and went flailing in the air before she fell face-first into the water. I rushed to her aid, worried she was injured and whether there'd be another trip to the hospital. She resurfaced, huffing and puffing.

"Are you okay?" I patted her shoulder checking for—something—broken bones.

Em nodded numbly. "Yeah."

Maya giggled and quickly covered her mouth. Em glared at her. The giggles turned into loud, shrill laughter, and in a blink of an eye, Maya was on the ground rolling, sputtering and clutching her stomach tightly as she bellowed. I couldn't hold in my giggles that morphed into uncontained laughter.

"What? What's happened?" Adam stood at the edge of the pool, arms on his hips, looking from Em and me in the pool to Maya who was still rolling on the ground.

"Em..." Maya wheezed. "She...she fell... She was like..." Maya tried to stand and failed, her laughter getting louder. "My stomach hurts." She wiped tears from her eyes and sniffed.

"It's not that funny." Em got out of the pool, grabbed a towel lying on a lounge chair, and pulled her cap off.

"It was that funny," Maya sighed.

"Bye. I'm leaving." Em stormed off.

Maya quickly sat up, the humor gone. "You're angry?"

"Sorry, Em." I called after her. Guilt swam in my head. She could have been hurt; and I was her tutor; the last thing I should have been doing was laugh at her mistakes. I shouldn't have—especially that hard.

"Sorry," Maya called after her.

Em ignored us and made a point of shutting the doors with a bang.

Maya chased after her. "Hold on. I'm sorry."

I watched them leave, unsure of how to soothe the feelings of a nine-year-old. "I've ruined it; I shouldn't have laughed. I broke a nine-year-old. How do I fix it?"

Adam shrugged. "She'll be fine. She'll forget in an hour. But you should know Em doesn't like being the butt of a joke."

"No one does."

"She gets really mad if you tease her. The good news—she forgets quickly. Don't get Maya angry though. You'll be giving her a revenge arc." He eased himself down and sat at the edge of the pool. "She hid my phone for a whole two days when I forgot their birthday."

"Cold of you." I swam closer.

"I was stressed by exams and all the stuff with Sarah."

"Sorry."

Adam splashed a little water my way and smiled. "I threatened her, but she acted like she was innocent.

Begged her, and she still played innocent. I had to bribe her to get it back."

"Alright, I'm definitely warned." I swam closer. Another few inches and I'd be between his legs, which wouldn't be a bad place to be if anyone asked. "What'd you bribe her with?"

"Donuts from Polly's. Works every time. That's how you get on their good side."

"Okay, I'll check it out."

Adam's eyes bugged out. "What? You've never been?"

"I don't think so." I'd never even heard of Polly's. We—Mo, Peep, Tani, and I—usually spent our money at a local diner that sold the most delicious sandwiches— thick, well stacked with soft bread and flavors that didn't leave your mouth for days.

"Rasheed, you've clearly not been living. You've never been to Polly's?" His voice had the same tone one would use if someone suggested fish could walk.

"No."

He stood up. "Come on, then; we have to go."

"What! Now?"

He nodded. "Yes. Before they close."

"But." I turned to the water, hoping an excuse would sprout from it.

"We'll get Em donuts, and then she'll forgive you."

"I guess." There was no time I'd ever said no to food, and I wouldn't start today. I got out of the pool and grabbed a fluffy white towel.

I turned to find Adam watching me. I was shirtless, my stomach exposed, a testament to how I was a couch potato. I flooded with heat, the embarrassment making me itch to turn away, too late. My skin prickled.

"What?" I twisted the towel in my hand. I'd punch him if he commented on my stomach—I swear it.

He swallowed, his Adam's apple bobbing up and down, and blinked. "I'll..." He pointed at the house. "...go tell Dad we're leaving while you get changed."

*

Mr. Herman's office faced the driveway, and the vibrations of his deep voice carried to the front porch where I sat waiting for Adam.

I remembered Mr. Herman as quiet and very orderly; he liked to cook and grill, and hated repeating himself. His presence usually caused me unease. Nothing personal, all dads had the same effect on me. It had taken me a while before I could comfortably be around Peep's dad, who had a haughty infectious laugh, and I was getting there with Mo's dad, who had good taste in movies. Eventually, I'd learned to be around Mr. Herman without wanting to mold myself to the wall.

Adam came out with a sour expression that he tried to smooth out with a small smile. "Let's do this."

We put my bike in the SUV's trunk, and I waited for Adam's comment about me not having a driver's license yet. I was getting there.

"You can play your music, if you like," Adam offered, which was generous. Mo usually needed a lot of ass-kissing before he let anyone play their music in his car.

I knew the song I wanted to play. I didn't like it, not anymore. It was too attached to cringeworthy memories of Adam, making it impossible to enjoy it. But with him here, I could concentrate on something else, like his lips, or his arms, taking the opportunity to imprint Adam's features in my mind. Once the opening beat started to pour out through the speakers, Adam cocked his head, pressing his lips together and tightening his grip on the steering wheel.

Another second passed before he broke into a reluctant grin. "If you're making fun of me, I hope your taste buds wither and die."

I laughed. "I'm not."

"Cool." He turned the volume up and started singing along to Owl City's "Good Time." He'd gotten shit from Izzy and Leo for liking this song, and Peep and I had jumped on the bandwagon. My excuse? I'd never pass up a chance to see Adam blushing. But it was cute how he sang the song under his breath without even noticing. It made my mind go fuzzy.

"This place," Adam said after the song ended. I turned to him. "It's absolutely top secret. You have to swear to keep it quiet. No one else can know. You cannot mention it to anyone."

"Doesn't that kill the point of their business?"

"Kind of, but I want to enjoy it before the lines get too long."

"You're such a brat."

"True." Adam glanced at me. "Are we clear? You'll honor this sacred deal?"

I nodded. "Deal."

Polly's Pastries was on Elm Avenue, where a beauty shop used to be. Tani had dragged us in there once to look for foundation, but the shop didn't stock her shade. The walls were white and decorated with framed paintings, the furniture was dark, and large potted plants sat in the corner of the shop. Instagram chic. Tani would love this place.

The guy behind the counter straightened and grinned, exposing brilliant white teeth fit for a toothpaste commercial. Totally unfair for a guy working in a pastry shop. "Hey," he said perkily.

Adam smiled back. "Hey, Kris. I brought a friend."

Kris took me in under a second. "That's nice," he said and turned his attention back to Adam. "Same old?" His voice was smooth like caramel. I frowned.

He was flirting with Adam!

Adam smiled. "Mhmm, and donuts for the twins. What about you, Rasheed?"

The pastries in the glass case looked good, delicious...but did Adam notice Kris was flirting, and was he encouraging it? Not that it was my business; color me a concerned citizen. "Kolaches?"

"Yes, good choice."

"You'll love it."

We took our seats in a cozy corner under a painting of a dog and cat lounging. Kris watched us walk away—watched Adam. Couldn't blame him; Adam had changed into black skinny jeans that molded to his body.

"What?" Adam asked.

"Kris likes you."

"What!" Adam whipped his head in Kris's direction—he was busy wiping the glass case—and turned back to me with a confused expression, his dark eyebrows pulled in at the center. "He doesn't."

"He was flirting with you."

Adam laughed. "He's being friendly."

"Pretty sure he wasn't."

Adam shrugged and took a bite.

I gaped at him. "Don't tell me you're that naive."

Adam frowned again. "Naive?"

I sighed. "Sorry. That was...mean." It wasn't like he was obliged to return crushes or notice them. That wasn't really any of his business. I guess I was a little bitter. "Sorry."

I grabbed the golden pastry and took a bite. The flavors of the bread mixed in with plum sauce melted in my mouth, and all that sweetness got absorbed into my heart. "Wow." I shut my eyes to savor the taste.

"Right?" Adam grinned triumphantly.

"So good." I took another bite that magnified. I groaned in pleasure. "I have to tell Tani about this place."

"If you break the deal, you'll owe me." Adam bit into his muffin and nodded in satisfaction.

"It was a premature deal." I eyed the muffin. "Can we trade bites?"

He pushed the muffin my way. "Sure."

I took a bite; it tasted like a warm spring day. "I feel robbed. Tani would love this. She is going to hate me when she finds out I knew."

"Who's Tani, by the way?"

"Peep's übersmart, überpretty girlfriend." I ran my tongue on the corner of my mouth to lick some of the sauce. Adam stared. I stopped. Bad table manners.

"Oh yeah, I've seen the pictures."

I leaned back once the last kolach was gone, spread my long legs, and patted my stomach. The dessert coupled with the swimming exercise was the perfect way to end my week. "That was good. I needed that."

"Long week?"

Every week seemed to be getting longer than the last. "Aha, I don't know if you heard, but Paul and Granma are getting married."

"What!" His eyebrows shot upward. "I haven't heard. Congratulations. That's cool."

I pressed my lips together.

"What? It's not?"

I sighed and ran my hands over my thighs. "It is, I guess. Okay, I'm not sure."

"'Cause she's too old?"

"No." I fiddled with a thread on my jeans. I'd worn my favorite ripped jeans, the only ones that hadn't faded and thinned from being old. "'Cause maybe the marriage won't work out."

"This is Paul from the hospital with that brown leather jacket?"

"Yeah, him."

Adam thought about it. "He seemed decent and looked like he cared about her."

I shook my head.

"What?"

"I remembered something. Liliana—"

"Which one? The tennis player?"

"The one who's in band."

"Go on."

"She totally liked you. She'd always comment and like your Facebook posts, and you never noticed it. You know, thinking about it I can name two more, Adriana and Kendall." Good to know I wasn't the only fool out there.

"Okay, but I was young then. It shouldn't count. What did you know when you were twelve?"

I rolled my eyes. "A lot actually. How can you not tell someone likes you?"

How could he have not seen *I* liked him? I'd gone from hiding his figurines, sometimes even his school books when he stepped on a nerve, to sharing my candy with him and making sure I always sat next to him. The only thing I hadn't done was put it on a T-shirt—and *tell* him, but that didn't count.

Adam cleared his throat. "Okay maybe I'm a bit aloof, and Paul is a really good actor."

I frowned. He did act like he cared for Granma. But I was worried about what would happen in the future. He might like her now, but what about later. Would he hurt her?

"Is there a reason you don't want her married?" Adam leaned closer.

"My grandfather was a bastard." Right, out with it. There was no need to sugarcoat it. "He treated her like shit."

That was an understatement. He abused her, and we moved to another continent to get away.

Adam's forehead creased. "Yeah, that's peak bastard behavior."

The memories rose, kicked open the locked memory box, and burst open. Babu Musa had beaten Granma every now and then because he believed in keeping her in check. The last time had been different; she'd ended up in the hospital, bruised face, fractured hand, broken ribs, and a concussion. Babu Rasheed, her oldest brother and the one I was named after, took us in before Frida whisked us away. Babu Musa came to visit after Granma was discharged. He showered us with apologies and me with toy cars, even though I preferred kitchen toys, much to his disgust. And when Granma said she wouldn't go back, the threats started. I remembered the sneer on his hard face, and the word *utajuta* spat from his mouth as if it was ingested venom.

I shivered and reached for the glass of water. We didn't wait to see if she would regret it.

"Maybe Paul is a good guy."

Maybe.

Chapter Twelve

During lunch break, on my way to see Mrs. Ballad about my college application, the most dreaded thing happened: I ran smack into Scott as I was taking a corner.

I opened my mouth to apologize and froze as I stared into eyes that were as blue as the ocean.

My gut tightened, my hand went limp, and I dropped the folder I'd been carrying. Someone kicked it, sending it spinning across the hall, the contents spilling out and scattered everywhere across the floor. A foot stepped on my stat notebook, smudging its cover decorated in tentacle doodles.

This was a nightmare.

Bile rose up my throat; I was going to vomit. Or die. The latter sounded like the best option.

I blinked, hoping he was an illusion I'd conjured. But no, he stood in front of me glowering—so close, I could make out the brown flecks in his blue eyes—and his mouth twisted in disgust.

Not a nightmare, only karma turning its wheel.

I'd gone over various things I could do when I saw Scott again: act nonchalant and finish my villainy arc, or show remorse and apologize. The second option was the right thing to do. My conscience knew it, but my throat had closed up and tongue turned to lead.

"Rasheed." Scott glared and turned his head heavenward. "Could this day get any worse?" He shook himself. "Nope. Screw this."

He shouldered past me, stopped, and stomped on top of my favorite purple pen—the one I used for hand-lettering in my bullet journal because nothing gave me more energy than seeing my to-do list in pretty cursive. The pen crunching made me wince. He twisted his thick black boot until the pen was nothing but bits and pieces. I stood there dumbfounded until a few shoves got me moving.

I stuffed my workbooks and papers, even the mangled purple pen, haphazardly into the folder. I needed to get out of there, and maybe to the moon, somewhere to process.

The second-best place was home, but it would be hours before I could return there.

There was no safe place in Brooksville High. I had to sieve through my thoughts to a soundtrack of laughter and loud conversation. It made it hard to think. I managed to assure myself that things weren't Armageddon-bad—except for the purple pen. The encounter also made clear to me how Scott felt; he hated me, no surprise there. He'd told me he loved me, and I'd ghosted him, and ignored all his messages assuring me it was okay if I wasn't ready to say it back.

I was a mess.

If each meet was like this, the year would be a disaster. At least Adam had been too swept up with Sarah to notice me.

*

After the Scott incident, the day got worse. Mrs. Ballard wasn't happy about my tardiness; in Calculus, we had a surprise quiz; and as I made my way on my bike to Mrs. Clay's place, a driver lost a little control and swerved, which made *me* swerve and nearly hit a tree.

"What's with you?" Mrs. Clay asked after I'd sighed one too many times.

I sighed—unable to help it—realized I'd done it again, and sighed once more. "Long day."

We were laying rocks for a zen garden design she'd found online. She'd go wild every time I got out of line, and therefore, preferred I handle the rock placement one at a time. It was boring work.

"And why was it long?"

I blinked.

Mrs. Clay hadn't taken an interest in my life, except maybe to chastise the current generation for being rotten, and all because she'd gone down the dairy aisle and found someone dancing.

"Some relationship stuff."

"I tend to enjoy that kind of drama."

I groaned. Not the D-word.

"Tell me."

"I was an ass to my ex, and I saw him for the first time today. He stomped on my favorite purple pen."

"That's not very nice."

It really wasn't.

"How were you an ass?" Mrs. Clay asked.

"I ghosted him."

She blinked at me. "And what is that supposed to mean?"

I sighed. "I stopped talking to him."

"That's not so bad."

"After he said the L-word."

"The L-word?" Mrs. Clay asked. "Love?"

"Mhmm. I freaked out…" I opened my mouth, but the words sat heavy on my tongue. No one had ever said they loved me. No one. Not even Granma, and I knew for sure she loved me. I swallowed the words, too personal, too embarrassing to share. Scott had overwhelmed me with the announcement, and I hadn't known how to react.

"Why would you be scared?"

"We were together for only four months."

"And you think there's a start date for when people can say they love each other?" Mrs. Clay shook her head. "You young ones. I met Felix at a movie theatre, and we spent the entire night together. A month later, we moved in together and stayed together for fifty-two years. You can't help feelings; they're instinctual." She paused as my mind took in her words. I marveled at them, the longest she'd ever spoken to me that weren't orders. "Did you love him?"

I frowned, worried my lower lip between my teeth. "I don't know."

"If you have to think about it, it's a no. But ignoring him after he opened up to you was unkind."

"I know."

"What do you plan to do?"

"Become one with the wind, and then he'll never see me again."

"That's very cowardly. Hmm, but I can't say I am surprised."

"You think I'm a coward?"

"I do."

I gaped.

"Oh, don't look at me like that. It's true. Now, are we done with the heartfelt conversation? Because I pay you by the hour, and my garden still needs work done."

*

Things were not better at home. Paul and Granma were huddled around her ancient Samsung tablet. Paul's hand was on Granma's knee. I gawked—okay, what was happening?

"What are you guys doing?" I asked, closing the door behind me.

"Looking at old pictures." Granma said. "Come see yourself." I stepped closer, and she handed me the tablet.

On the screen was an eight-year-old me, skinny, face hollow, with wide, round eyes that looked like they would fall out if someone shook me too hard. I was standing in front of our old house, dressed in what had to be a Christmas outfit, matching denim jacket and jeans with a SpongeBob T-shirt, my thumbs held up for the camera.

"Ulikuwa mdogo."

I *was* young, small too. And sickly. I always managed to have a runny nose even in Mombasa's hot climate. "I'm grown now."

Thank the gods I'd hit a growth spurt and went from five foot to six foot almost overnight. The basketball coach had even shown an interest in me. He'd asked me to join the team and promptly kicked me out when he realized I couldn't dribble a ball to save my life—and do it while running? How?

I kicked my backpack to the side and settled on the floral armchair. I flipped to the next picture of me and

Granma cutting a cake, another at Babu Rasheed's house, celebrating Ramadan, a picture of Frida in her graduation gown, another of me at the beach posing with other kids. Good times. Another swipe and I found myself staring at a picture of me and Babu Musa on the red couch Granma had loved so much. Babu Musa was a tall, skinny man with a dark moustache and a long face framed with hollow cheeks. His moustache was unsettling—two thick caterpillars perched on his upper lip—and it made my skin crawl.

"I didn't know you had these," I said, looking up.

"Frida went back to the house to get them and other things before we left the country."

Speaking of the same, she appeared. The vest she wore left her arms exposed, and her left one was covered in a sleeve tattoo made to look like the arm was robotic—it seemed fitting somehow.

"Rasheed, hey!"

But why did she always have to say my name like she was surprised at my existence, every time!

"Hey, Frida," I said.

"Food's ready."

Granma pushed off her seat, and Paul placed a hand on her arm, stopping her. "You don't have to get up; let me do it for you."

"Oh, Paul, I've been seated the whole day."

He rubbed his hand up her arm. "I guess you have."

He helped Granma up and ushered her to the kitchen, which had to be less than three steps away. Granma made a weird sound. Frida blinked.

Okay that was it. Granma and I needed to have a talk.

I missed the plot of the drama, my mind locked on Paul and Granma. They sat very close to each other on the sofa, her floral armchair abandoned in favor of Paul who exchanged quiet murmurs with her. He stayed for tea, and even after that was done, he stayed a while longer—long enough I managed to finish outlining an essay assignment.

I headed to Granma's room as soon as Paul left. She sat on the edge of her monstrous four-poster bed that belonged in the fifties, wrapped in a thick, brown-green robe, flipping through the notebook Tani had given her.

"You're not working on that crazy idea, are you?" I asked.

"I don't find it crazy. I quite like it."

"It has too much going on."

"Doesn't life?"

I lingered before I took a step into the room. I jumped right into it. "Look, are you sure about Paul?"

She shut the book and set it aside. "Yes, I'm sure." She frowned. "You don't like him?"

"Um, well, he's fine...I guess. How can we be sure he *is* trustworthy?" And not pretending. Even Babu Musa had his moments; he'd buy Granma lavish presents occasionally.

"Because Paul has a gentle soul."

A heavy weight pressed down on my shoulders.

She patted the space next to her. I settled there, and she turned to me. "I know you're thinking about your grandfather, but Paul is not him; that's one thing I'm sure about." She considered me. "You know, it wouldn't be fair to me if I kept myself from enjoying life because something bad happened. Learn from it? Absolutely. Life has so much going on, Rasheed, so much, and whatever happened back then, it's done. We can't go back. We can only look forward. This, with Paul—" She huffed. "It makes me happy, and I want to hold on to that feeling."

I said nothing, stunned by the candidness.

"If things change, I'll leave. It's a promise I made to myself, and now I'm making it to you."

The earnestness in her eyes warmed me. "Promise me it won't get to be as bad as last time."

"It won't, I assure you."

"Okay..." I fisted my hands and then released them. "Does he know I'm gay?"

"I haven't told him. I respect your wish to let you do your own coming out at your own time."

That was because she kept saying "my gay grandson" every time she referenced me after I'd come out to her. It annoyed me that I wasn't just a grandson anymore—oh, no, my status had been elevated to gay grandson, and this new level came with curious stares and awkward silences. So I'd asked her politely to not be announcing my gayness to everyone. It was none of their business.

"But Paul is no homophobe," she continued. "I wouldn't tolerate him otherwise. Do you want me to tell him?"

"No, I'll do it myself." So I could see his reaction.

After a stretch, Granma spoke. "If *you* are unsure, tell me, and I'll call off the wedding."

"You'd do that?"

She smiled and patted my shoulder. "Yes. Without a doubt."

My throat clogged with thick emotion. Granma had never said it, but I understood she cared for me. Not because she'd had no option after Frida left me with her. Not because it was the right thing. She genuinely liked me.

Maybe I was being irrational. "I'll...I'll think about it."

She eyed my hair before lifting a hand to touch it. "And you need a haircut."

I ducked and passed my fingers through the short curls. I normally had a Jordan cut. It made me appear like a man on a mission, but the extra inches softened my features. "I'm liking it long."

"Hmm," she said with her lips pinched. "It's not a terrible look."

I scoffed. "Thanks, Granma."

"You're welcome, and I'm glad you came to me. Do it more often."

"I will." I pointed at the notebook. "Tell me more about what you're working on."

Granma brightened and started explaining the vision she had for her story. Somehow it had gotten even worse; for some unexplained reason, there was a talking horse acting as a spirit guide. At that point, it became hard to hold back the giggles. She kicked me out of her room mumbling something about my lack of imagination.

Chapter Thirteen

To celebrate the end of the week, my people and I were going out to eat, a burger maybe or a pizza, depending on the mood. What I wanted was to go back to Polly's Pastries. The only problem was the "deal" with Adam.

An idea popped into my head. I grinned at its genius. I started typing. *Remember our deal?*

The reply was immediate. We'd been texting the entire week, catching up, trading memes and consoling each other about schoolwork.

ADAM: *the one you swore not to break??*

ME: *yeah...*

ADAM: *what about that deal that I hold very dear to my heart?*

ME: *you should have joined drama club*

ADAM: *me willingly subject myself to a mob?*

ME: *it's called a crowd*

ADAM: *the deal...*

ME: *Mo, Peep, Tani, and I are going out to eat ...*

ADAM: *you wouldn't*

ME: *exactly I wouldn't*

ADAM: *exactly because we value trust in this new friendship and you wouldn't want to jeopardize that.*

ME: *true*

ME: *but hear me out... I could invite you and I wouldn't technically be breaking the deal because you'll be there?*

ME: *also friends hang out together?*

Soon as the text went out, I realized I had asked Adam out! Me! My dating game was weak. I heavily relied on the invisible hand of the universe to put things into place, like a group assignment bringing me together with the crush or the person of interest being ballsy.

ADAM: *lmao...I'll see you there.*

ME: *cool*

"What are you smiling at?" Mo asked as I got into his Chevy. Peep and Tani were squeezed in the back. I was sure they didn't mind having to sit nearly on top of each other.

"I came out of the factory like this," I said.

Mo snorted.

I winced at the jab of a knee in my back. "Your knee is making me uncomfortable," I told Peep.

"It's this clown car."

Peep shifted in the back, lodging his knee properly against a tender spot on my spine.

"Dude you couldn't get an adult car?" I grumbled.

"Fuck off. First, I won't take shit from you when you don't know how to drive," Mo said. "And second, I didn't get this car to give free rides. It was for me and my girl."

"Yet," I mumbled. I was going to learn, soon.

In the back, Tani snorted. "What girl?"

"The one who was supposed to be seated in the front seat with a hand on my—"

"Ew," Tani said.

"—thigh. I was going to say thigh. And hey, I have to watch you and Peep make out, every now and then, which is the grossest thing on earth."

Peep flicked Mo's ear.

"I'm saying," Mo went on. "It's like you eat her whole face with that big-ass mouth of yours."

Tani laughed. "I told you, you do that."

"You told me you liked it," Peep said. "Wait, you don't like it?"

"As long as you're a cute little puppy, I don't mind," Tani said sweetly.

"What?" Peep said, sounding wounded.

"It means she doesn't like it, bro," Mo supplied.

"Sorry, babe," Tani said and planted a loud kiss on Peep's cheek.

*

Kris was still behind the counter and didn't seem to recognize me. Ouch. Like, bro, I was here last week. Maybe Adam had a habit of bringing people to Polly's, and Kris couldn't be bothered. It annoyed me either way.

I got the chocolate cake, and we went to sit. This time, the place was crowded and a little noisy. We spied an empty booth in the back and made our way to it. I made sure Mo got in first, so when Adam came, he'd have to sit next to me.

Tani cooed and jumped with excitement about how delicious her pie was. "This is so good!"

"You're welcome."

"How'd we not know about this place 'til now?"

"It opened at the beginning of the summer," said Paul as he read from his phone. "It's had so many positive reviews and only one bad one." He snorted. "The bad one says the place is not 'family friendly' because of the painting of two women passionately kissing."

"What a prude."

The moment Adam walked in, my whole body buzzed with awareness. He stood in line, wearing gray jeans, a white shirt, and a denim jacket. He scanned the crowd; I straightened and waited for him to notice me. When he did, a giant grin split his features, and my heart flatlined before it picked up again in a loud, steady rhythm. I smiled back.

Kris served Adam with a flirtatious smile, and Adam ate it up. I rolled my eyes. There was no way he did not notice that.

Finally, he made his way toward us.

"Adam!" Peep said with excitement. He got up and hugged Adam.

"Nice to see you." Adam clapped Peep's back with affection.

"See, Kris was flirting," I said when I had Adam's attention. "You saw it this time."

He grinned. "Okay, you were right."

I was glad Adam had come, he and Mo gushed about their favorite animes and mangas. He and Tani found out they were both obsessed with Spiderman. He asked Peep about his doodling, and I looked on, happy to have his thigh pressed to mine and the glances he threw my way every now and then.

*

"There's a used bookshop on this street; we have to go," Mo said as we got up to leave. It was the last thing we wanted to hear, high from sugar and good conversation. We collectively groaned.

"I think you should read the ones you bought last time," Peep said.

"I did read them," said Mo. "I don't ask much from—"

"We're going, save the speech," I said.

"Aww, I improved it from last time... I added the part where my cat died."

The book thrift shop was a good ten-minute walk from Polly's. The narrow pavements didn't allow all of us to walk in the same row. Mo stuck with Peep and Tani at the front, his arm swung around Tani's shoulder to piss her off. Adam and I followed behind at a slower pace, arms brushing every now and then, rattling my heart with excitement. Was this a date? The thought made me nervous. It was equivalent to standing on the edge of a cliff, and I was scared of falling.

Adam and Mo drifted to the comics and manga section. Peep sat down on an old leather sofa at the front of the shop and pulled out his phone. Tani and I went to the magazine section. She picked up a gossip magazine, and we crowded to see who had done what and with who.

"So, you and Adam." Tani flipped a page and peered at me through her eyelashes. She had long eyelashes she'd dyed navy-blue. She wore blue eyeliner on her lower eyelid and shiny lip gloss reapplied before we left the bakery. Her dark skin was flawless. She distracted me for a moment.

"It's not like that." Heat crawled up my face, and my lips twitched. It kind of *was* like that, from my end at least.

"It looked like that. You were glued to his side."

I laughed, embarrassed. "The booth was small. He's just a touchy-feely guy. He's straight."

"He tell you that?"

"No, but—" I glanced to where the comic shelves were. I couldn't see him, but I could hear the rumble of his voice and Mo fawning over the selections. Once I'd been convinced there could be something between us with the way he would look at me, like I was a painting he was trying to make sense of, and the small touches, a hand on my knee, an arm slung over my shoulder. Once he'd brushed a fallen eyelash from my cheek...but he'd gone on to date Sarah. I shrugged. "It doesn't matter. We're friends." Which was true.

"Very close friends, I noticed." Tani smirked.

"I'm serious." She didn't believe me, couldn't blame her; my whole face was twitching with nerves. "I'm gonna check out the photography books."

"You're totally running away from the conversation. Fine, I'll be here drooling over these shirtless dudes." She flicked a finger over a guy advertising underwear.

He did look good, a full six-pack, large pecs, and that *V*. But no, I needed a break. A moment to compose myself and purge thoughts of Adam. Couldn't have her filling my head with hope when I liked it desolate and bleak.

"Hey, I was looking for you." The voice skirted over my skin, causing the hairs to rise. Adam walked toward me and plucked the book I'd been mindlessly flipping through from my hand. "Hmm."

I extended my hand to grab the book back, but he moved it out of my reach.

He smiled triumphantly and handed it back. "Here."

"You think you're slick, huh?"

"I know I am."

I took the book and put it back on the shelf.

"Why'd we stop being friends?"

My heart stuttered. My mind tried to grasp at anything. "We grew apart, I guess." Which was true, a part of it. I couldn't explain me feeling betrayed by him in the aisle of a bookshop.

"You and Peep didn't." Sadness crowded his eyes. Guilt washed over me. I was so going to throw up.

I chewed on the inside of my cheek to keep from blurting the wrong thing. "Peep and I went to the same church." Back when I went to church.

Adam gave me a blank stare. Okay, that was a shit reason.

Tani turned the corner. She wiggled her eyebrows in a suggestive way and smirked.

I ignored her and decided to use her presence as an escape from the conversation with Adam. "Oh, are we leaving?"

Coward, a voice hissed. I couldn't deny it. Even then, I didn't think there would ever be a time I could come clean about me being jealous. Ever. It was mortifying.

"I guess. I'm buying this." She waved the Men's Health. "I think the ladies at the retirement village will like it for scrapbooking."

"Cool! Tani goes to visit the elderly; isn't that sweet?" I explained to Adam as we walked back to the front of the store, and rumbled some more about how Tani liked interacting with the elderly.

Peep was where we'd left him. "Mo, we're leaving; you better not be reading," he called out as he stretched.

"Yes, Dad!" Mo called back. Mo came back carrying two books and headed for the counter.

Peep, Adam, and I decided to wait outside, which turned out to be a miscalculation because Adam blurted out, "Peep, why did we stop hanging out?"

Peep's gaze found mine before it fixed on Adam. "We got busy. I got into art, Rasheed with school clubs." I'd joined every club that would have me, and sport—there weren't many, I was shit at nearly all sports except swimming. During that time, none of us hung out for several weeks. Peep and I got back together because he had to tutor me in chemistry, but Adam drifted further from reach. "And you started dating, and we couldn't find time to meet up."

"Oh." Adam frowned.

"It happens." Peep clapped him on the shoulder.

"I had fun today," said Adam.

"Yeah, glad you came."

Mo and Tani came back with their bags, and I escorted Adam to his car. There was an awkward pause when he opened the car door and our eyes snagged on each other. I wanted nothing more than to wrap my arms around him and bury myself in his neck. I pushed the thought away and settled for a smile. He grinned and promised to text, got in his car and drove off.

I caught up to Peep. "Thanks for that."

"You're welcome; didn't do it for you though. Adam was my friend too. We did hang out afterwards when you wouldn't, remember?"

"Yeah." The clubs and being a water boy gave me all the excuses I needed to miss their get-togethers. Seeing Adam had been hard and seeing him and Sarah, all nice and cozied, even worse. I'd needed some space.

"I was definitely a third wheel. They way they'd look at me as if they couldn't wait for me to leave so they'd be alone." Oh, I remembered that. "This one time we were at his place and Sarah went to the bathroom, and Adam stood outside the door waiting." He laughed.

"Did he though?"

"Nah. But he kept looking at the hallway, waiting for her to come back."

I lightly checked him. "Next time you ask me to hangout, only you and Tani and me, remember that feeling."

Chapter Fourteen

The twins stood before me with wide grins, and, thank God, different one-pieces with the same floral design. One was green, and the other was orange. "Glad to see your swimsuits are different," I said and earned giggles. "But let's do introductions to refresh my memory."

Em, I think, in green, rolled her eyes and pointed at her sister in orange. "Every time. Maya is the talkative one—"

"Hey!"

"And I'm the quiet one." She pointed with pride at herself.

"I'm not talkative," Maya protested. "Dad calls it networking and resourceful."

"Right." I pointed to the one in green. "Em." Then to the twin in orange. "Maya." I clapped my hands together. "Okay, let's do this. We start with stretches."

They weren't into the stretching today, exaggerating their movements and making sounds to show how exerting the task was.

"But why do we have to do this?" Maya asked.

"So your muscles don't ache. Now pull your legs apart."

"When do we get to the fun stuff?"

"Soon. First, we perfect the headfirst dive."

"We only wanted to know how to dive like the twin boys in the video, not join the Olympics," Em moaned.

Kids, they'll tear you apart. No wonder the teachers at school looked soulless.

A while later, Adam and his friend, Eric—the one in a band shirt I'd seen him with—joined us. After a quick hello, Eric deposited himself on the lounge chair and melted into the background.

"Have they worn you down yet?" Adam asked.

"Who me? Never," I said in a hoarse voice. The twins really weren't into it, and I'd had to repeat myself short of a million times. I was thirsty, and the sun beating down on us was draining the last reserve of my energy. Behind their backs, I mouthed, *Help me!*

"Pizza is here; you hungry?"

"Yes!" they said at the same time and got out of the pool. I ducked under the water, swam to the edge of the pool, and pulled myself out. Adam stared at me as if I'd grown an extra arm out of my abdomen.

"What?"

"Nothing." He threw a towel my way. "Get yourself cleaned up."

When I got back freshly showered, Eric was leaving. Natalie was seated on a stool by the breakfast bar, a Kindle in hand, Mr. Herman with a glass of wine next to her, and the twins were browsing through Netflix while Adam helped himself to a large slice of pizza.

"That boy never talks," Natalie said. "What do y'all say to each other?"

I slid next to Adam, and he handed me a plate of pizza. "We play video games; talking is distracting."

Mr. Herman huffed. "You should look for more productive friends."

"Yes, Dad," Adam sighed. "Though Eric *is* productive."

"And stop being a yes-man and start walking the talk. Get rid of that gaming console and start spending more time doing things that build you."

My eyes flickered to Adam; his nose crinkled in irritation. "I don't spend all day playing video games."

"It sure looks that way from where I'm standing."

"I help Eric test the game he's working on. I'm helping with the character development. And I help manage Izzy's calendar."

Mr. Herman shook his head. "That's well and good, but you need to stand on your own two feet instead of piggybacking off others' accomplishments."

"Michael," Natalie said in a low voice. "Let him do what makes him happy. He's seventeen. He has a whole life ahead to figure everything out."

Adam's grip on his plate tightened. "I'll be in my room?"

"Okay, baby," Natalie said sweetly.

Adam carelessly placed his plate on the desk when we got to his room, the pizza slice sliding to the edge of the plate and the pepperoni starting to slip off it. He threw himself on Izzy's bed. "Ugh."

"Looks like your dad reads too much self-help."

"Just the one— 'Mastering your Life by Planning your Future in Eight Steps.' He found it in the airport and read it on his flight. He never shuts up about how it changed his life." Adam sighed and stood, then knelt on the carpet, the sweats cupping and stretching over his ass. Holy shit! Look away! Now...my eyes remained glued to his ass until sweat started to pool in my armpits. My dick was taking notice and liking it.

Adam straightened and produced a dusty book. He handed it to me, and I shook myself from the trance. "Here's the book. He gave me a copy, but I couldn't get past the front page."

I picked it up and flipped to the front page.

In life, you're either the wolf or the sheep. This book shows you how to be the wolf.

I laughed. "Not the shepherd?"

"There's a chapter dedicated to that, but I didn't read it."

"I remember he used to be kind of laid-back."

"He was. Now, he has an assessment of everything we do. Everything is worked out in spreadsheets. It can be kind of suffocating." Adam sat up, reached for the slice of pizza, and took a bite. "Mom says it's the stress of starting his own company, and I'm, like, he should take a break, but apparently rest is for the weak. There's a chapter there— 'The Leisure Myth' or something."

I chewed on my pizza. "Sorry."

He sighed. "I miss when we'd sit and watch ESPN. Now, we can't be in the same room for too long without him devolving into a lecture."

"I hate when they do that." I'd learned my lesson from sharing any jokes with Granma.

"Now imagine that's, like, all our conversations." He cracked his knuckles. "There's...stuff...I'd like to tell him, but I don't know. I'm not sure how he'd take it."

"It's that bad?"

Adam chewed slowly. "On my part, yes."

"Why? What is it?" I thought back to the Sarah and Adam rumors. The words stumbled out before I could get ahold of my tongue. "Oh my God, is this about Sarah?" I paused. "I mean, sorry. It's none of my business."

"Sarah's supposed abortion?" Adam laughed. "God, no. Ugh, that's some stupid thing some idiot said."

"So it's not true?"

"Hell, no. Did you believe it?"

I shrugged. "I've heard crazier things."

"It wasn't that. Damn, if mom heard that, she'd go crazy and bury me alive. I'd never risk it. Can't even imagine what Dad would do."

"Help dig the grave?" A slice of pepperoni landed on my lap as I went to take a bite.

"Yes, that." Adam handed me a Kleenex with a smirk. "You have charming table manners."

"I try, but I also have immeasurable self-control as I have chosen not to ask what the tissues are for." It wouldn't do my mind any good to build images in my head.

"I'm not embarrassed. We can talk about it."

"But we won't. Let's get back to why you and Sarah broke up."

"She said she doesn't like me the same anymore, and she can't stay in a relationship where the feelings are dead."

Their relationship had been on a pedestal. They'd liked each other, cared for each other. Everyone was sure they'd end up married with three kids.

"But you were in love and stuff."

"We were, I guess, but one day we weren't." He cracked his knuckles. "After we broke up, I thought I was okay with it, but one day, I found myself crying like a bitch because my heart was aching."

"Sorry."

"I'm doing better now. I'm planning on staying single as long as I was in a relationship, to try this single life."

Oh. That was oddly disappointing.

Adam twirled a pen, put it down, and reached for his phone. He connected to the speaker, and EDM started to play. EDM with no lyrics.

"This is my least favorite kind of music, you know that?"

"I was testing something." He grinned. "I knew this friendship was doomed to last." He swiped through the phone, and a lady with a mournful voice started to croon about how she wasn't going to burn the memories. "Better?"

"Yeah." I fell back on the bed and listened to her, eyes closed, enjoying the intimacy.

"So..."

I looked at him through hooded eyelids. Too lazy to lift my head. Sleep was a few blinks away. He bit his lower lip and let it go smoothly. I followed the movement as the heat pooled down lower. I parted my lips. I needed to get this back on track. "Yeah? So?"

"The thing I want to tell my dad but can't..." Adam regarded me. I straightened. "I'm bisexual."

The world was drowned out by the rush of blood in my ears, and I became aware only of my beating heart and the words echoing in my mind. "What?" I croaked, sitting up.

"Yeah."

OhmyGod. OhmyGod. Remember to breathe. I exhaled, releasing the breath I was holding. I must have stepped into another dimension where daydreams came true. "You're into guys?"

Adam bit his lower lip.

Questions raced through my mind. Too fast, I couldn't latch onto one. Where to start?

Calm down Rasheed.

"Umm, uh, wow, that's cool."

Adam smiled. I was radiating awkward. I was gay; why was this difficult to process? "Found out this year. Well, I think I knew before." He huffed a laugh. "Only, my mind couldn't rationalize it. I kept going back and forth with it."

At seven, watching soaps with Granma, I'd come to the realization I wanted to fall in love with the handsome male actors. My dreams involved men, never girls. I'd had my first kiss in kindergarten with a boy behind the school building. It had taken a while before I understood the meaning of gay and before I could be comfortable with it.

"Imagine Dad finding out two of his sons are into guys."

"He won't like it?"

"Maybe. What I know for sure is that it will build another wall between us. He's already up my ass about being lazy; now, I'm bi?" His shoulders slumped. "I don't want to hide it though. It's always sitting at the tip of my tongue. I've only told only Eric, and it feels nice to be honest about it."

"Maybe ask Wally for some advice then? He's been there with coming out with your dad."

"I've been thinking about that too. If I see him—he's an EMT now."

"That's awesome."

"You had a crush on him, right?"

I laughed. "You're so blind, I can't even. I didn't have a crush on Wally; it was hero worship."

"If you had the chance to date Wally, would you take it?"

"I still didn't have a crush on him...but yeah."

"Why?"

I shrugged. I once had an entire page in my diary where I praised Wally for being out and proud. In some way, he had inspired me to come out. "He's nice."

"Nice. Really, that's all? That's what made you follow him around?"

"What do you want me to say?"

"Some deep shit. Everyone knows Wally is nice and near perfect."

"Jealous?"

Adam laughed. "Fuck no, everyone knows I'm better-looking."

"Everyone knows Izzy is the best-looking."

"Been rating us, have you?"

I rolled my eyes at his smug tone. "Everyone rates you guys."

Which was a stupid thing to say because the conversation could only have gone one way from there.

"How'd you rank me?"

The first thing that came to mind was: one.

"That high, huh?" Adam said when I didn't reply.

"You wish," I said, but the words felt weak on my tongue.

Adam was bisexual. Adam liked guys. Adam could like me.

A thrill of excitement shot down my spine, and hope swelled in my chest.

No. No. I couldn't think like that.

The line between us had become thinner, sure, but this could possibly make the situation worse for me. What if I developed a serious crush, and he didn't reciprocate it? I'd be wrecked. I'd have to keep it clean. No lingering glances, no staring at certain body parts, and definitely *no feelings.*

Chapter Fifteen

Saturday mornings were no longer quiet affairs. The sound of laughter melded with the shrill of a drill, the vacuum running, and the hum of the washing machine.

We'd doubled the number of people in one weekend, and it was disorienting. Paul was now a fixture in my life. He was always over and, at least, keeping himself useful; he'd taken the broken armchair apart and was in the process of fixing it. I wanted to talk to him, but I hadn't caught him alone yet. If Granma wasn't with him, then Frida was.

I could almost understand Adam's frustration at having so many siblings.

I yawned, scratching my belly with one hand while I scrolled through social media with the other, hoping for something interesting. Mo had posted a full picture of him and Malia, and Tani had bought a new lipstick she was raving about.

I then checked my to-do list—normally I'd write it in my bullet journal, with the purple pen, but I couldn't look at it without thinking about Scott—and realized, with great satisfaction, I was done...with everything except one. At the bottom of the list I'd added Scott's name with a question mark at the end. I hadn't run into him due to luck and fast skills when it came to ducking as soon as I saw the pink hair tips. It was pathetic.

Frida joined me in the laundry area. We exchanged a "morning," and I followed her motions from the corner of my eye as she started stacking the shelves. Unease settled in the room and in my mind, making it hard to concentrate on my phone. I didn't know how to be around her without thoughts of inadequacy worming in.

Was it my fault she'd never been motherly toward me?

"There's some *mahamri*, if you like."

"Oh, you made them?"

"Mom wouldn't keep quiet about how much she missed them." She glanced my way, her eyes never quite meeting mine.

"She missed them. That's what she was making when—when she had the attack." I shifted my weight from my left foot to the right, unsure of what else to say. Dialogues with Frida mainly consisted of what, why, where. The replies were usually monosyllabic and, if stretched, one or two sentences. I swear Siri and I had more interesting conversations.

What could we talk about anyway? I'd tried to ask about her travels and documentaries, but she always answered through gritted teeth.

"What food do you miss?"

I stilled and studied Frida. I could only make out her side profile. Her eyes were fixed on the shelves and her face blank of any emotion. I could not point to a time she'd shown any interest in getting to know me, especially not as a teenager. Last time she'd shown interest out of the ordinary was shortly after we moved in with her. But she'd left and come back colder than the Arctic.

I turned my focus to the question she'd asked. "Umm, I guess *achari* and *Babu Kachri*."

Frida's face did a thing where she seemed excited—her eyes widened, and her lips twitched. "That's bringing back memories. I loved *Babu Kachri* when I was in university. I remember the long queues under the sun to get some. I think we can make some." She rubbed her earlobe, then let her hand drop. "If you like, that is. I can show you how to make it..."

My eyebrows shot up. As in me and her. Spending time *together*. Thoughts swirled as I tried and failed to make sense of it. Was she serious?

"Okay, that's...yeah."

The corner of her mouth twitched. "You choose the date."

"Okay." I swiped around my phone and opened my calendar, marked with assignment due dates, test dates, and various events Peep was always trying to get me to attend. "Umm, when are you going back?" Back. Because she hardly stayed.

Frida straightened, crossed her arms, and stared at the wall with the crumbling paint. "I got fired."

My jaw dropped. "You got fired?" From the job you invested in more than you ever did me?

She shrugged. "Apparently, I was underperforming." Bitterness laced her words.

"When was this?"

"A few weeks ago."

My eyes narrowed. A few weeks ago? And no one had bothered to tell me. And she hadn't come straight to us. It was so typical. I fisted my hands. "So where were you when I called?"

"In Greece."

Of course. Anywhere but where I was. The thought left a bitter taste in my mouth. "I'll text you when I'm free."

"Okay."

*

Adam's texts were waiting for me when I was done with Lucy's garden. Lucy was my other client, making two so far. Mrs. Clay had recommended me to her, though I wondered how Mrs. Clay had got a word in—Lucy loved talking about her son, Albert. Somehow, every conversation circled back to Albert. We would be talking about which row to plant garlic, and suddenly, I'd be hearing a detailed explanation about Albert's career as a scientist. I was helping Lucy with her vegetables, and unlike Mrs. Clay, she was decided on what she wanted and how she wanted it.

ADAM: *are you free?*

ADAM: *taking the twins to go see a movie*

ADAM: *we'll go for food later, I'm buying…*

ADAM: *forgot you are a responsible person with a job txt me when you're done.*

I smiled.

ME: *I'm done now, offer still stands?*

ADAM: *yes! Starts in 20 but don't rush*

The movie theater was a good fifteen-minute bike ride. Lucy lived on a commercial street, which she mentioned Albert loved to complain about because of the noise.

My eyes landed on Adam's the moment I stepped into the brick building, and we grinned at each other like idiots. The smile grew wider the closer I got to him, and butterflies in my stomach fluttered harder.

Red flags went up in my mind.

Clearly, I was setting myself up for disaster. I shouldn't have come.

"You came!" squealed Maya. She hugged me, only coming to my stomach, and pulled away before I could react.

"Yeah."

Em gave me an awkward "Hey," and Adam squeezed my shoulder.

"What's this movie about?" I asked.

"A teen movie," said Adam.

"We heard there was a cute boy."

"Aren't you too young for that?" Adam asked them.

"That doesn't mean we don't have eyes," they said at the same time and then folded their hands, also at the same time. Both of them realized they were doing the same thing and glared at each other, dropping their hands. At the same time.

"I'm going to buy gum," huffed Em.

Adam shook his head. "Don't buy gum. No way am I going to watch a bad storyline *and* hear you chew at the same time."

"You don't know it'll be bad," protested Maya.

"You're right; it couldn't be as bad as the PG-rated horror from last time." He turned to me. "It was so bad."

"And you think we liked to hear you complain for a whole month?" Maya rolled her eyes.

"You like to whine a lot," Em said.

Adam grinned at me. "You said you wanted siblings, right? Take them away so I can finally live out my fantasy of being an only child."

That earned a shove from Maya, and I laughed.

The movie was about a girl falling in love with a ghost. The guy playing the ghost had a magnificent jawline that managed to distract from the slow pacing.

"Sorry for making you suffer, I wasn't strong enough to do it by myself," whispered Adam. His breath was cool on my cheek from the milkshake he was drinking—a chocolate milkshake, believe it, but I chose to overlook that offence.

I turned to face him. He was close enough I could make out most of his face. The light from the screen illuminated his right side and did a fantastic job of highlighting his lips. I glanced down at them, the darkness making me bold.

I squeezed my eyes shut. This was where I needed to practice self-control.

"I don't mind."

"I feel for Leo. He had to sit through every shark movie we could find as kids," Adam said.

"Oh yeah. I remember that." I chuckled.

Adam leaned even closer. "Wish mom would sit through one of these movies so she wouldn't have to insist too much about me accompanying them."

"Oh, ah, yeah. Your mom was supposed to come over today for the book club."

Adam snorted. "It's her excuse to get out of the house."

"And Granma's excuse to entertain. She likes visitors. Back in Mombasa, she always had someone over, family or neighbor."

"Have you been back?"

"No, Granma's always talking about it when things get tough, but I don't think she ever means it." This happened at the end of most months when the bills came in.

Maya shushed us. We smiled at each other and turned back to the screen.

My phone buzzed.

ADAM: *I want to sleep…*

I glanced at him. He pretended to nod off. I bit my lip to stop from laughing.

ME: *I'm sure there'll be a shirtless scene*

ME: *of the dude…*

ME: *maybe the girl too?*

ME: *but it's mostly always the guy…*

Next to me, Adam snorted. Lord spare me from making a fool of myself.

ADAM: *abs are nice, but I think I'm more into softness*

I swallowed thickly.

ME: *that's nice.*

There was a long beat.

ADAM: *what kind of guys are you into?*

I started to sweat at the implication of the question. From experience, the conversation usually took this route if someone was interested in more and wanted to know if there was a chance of anything happening. But Adam had only recently discovered his bisexuality and could be asking out of curiosity.

Or both.

I bit my lip, pushed the thought aside, and concentrated on answering the question.

My relationship history was tragically short and devoid of any great romance. I'd dated four guys. Owen. I dated him the summer of freshman year when my infatuation with Adam had waned. A two-week affair that ended when we butted heads about a movie. After Owen, there was Rain, who was sweet but got bored with me after a month. Niko was my third. He was a fanfic writer. Our relationship started online but hadn't survived our real-life meet up. Then Scott, my most solid relationship.

Owen had been gangly and obsessed with cars, Rain was a tennis player with long hair that could be tied in a bun, Niko was boney and loved being on Quora, and Scott was average-looking and loved makeup.

The only striking similarity between them was that, somehow, they were all left-handed.

ME: *turns out I like left-handed people*

Adam started shaking with laughter. His deep rumbles found their way under my skin making my blood sing with delight. Maya shushed him.

"I've never heard of that one," he whispered. "So if a right-handed person tried to date you?"

"Trust me, my dating pool is too small to reject anyone." I only broke them after I started dating them.

"You realize I'm left-handed?" His lips brushed my ear and made my toes curl.

I closed my eyes and tightened my hold on the popcorn.

Drunk on the intimacy of the theatre, the cover of darkness, his warm breath on my skin that made it tingle, the idea that we might be flirting, I turned and said, "I do."

His breath hitched. He was close, our lips nearly touching. All I had to do was tip my head forward, and our mouths would be pressed together. Anticipation caused my heart to rattle in its ribcage.

This was real; his warm breath prickling my skin confirmed it.

Someone snorted, then burst into laughter and shattered the moment. Adam pulled back, and I grabbed a handful of popcorn and stuffed my mouth.

My pulse was racing. My clothes clung to my skin, and my armpits were sticky and wet.

Shit.

Long after the movie had ended, I still thrummed with awareness, while I tried to reason with myself that this couldn't happen again. Because, most likely, it would end up in a disaster, and I didn't have time for that.

Chapter Sixteen

My phone buzzed. I peeked at it and saw I had a text from Peep and noted it was twenty minutes past seven. Frida and I should have started making *Babu Kachri* by now. I couldn't help think she had chickened out and broken into hives at the thought of spending time with me— *I* was about to break into hives. Or maybe she was held up wherever she'd gone to.

Whatever the reason, I was anxious. Anxious that she would cancel, and partially hoping she would spare us the awkward that would no doubt be part of the evening.

I glanced back at the screen as it lit up with a second notification. A second text from Peep.

> PEEP: *I want to buy Tani a promise ring, is that insane?*

> MO: *why would you want to do that?*

> ME*: I think it's cute*

> PEEP: *okay let's hear it Mo*

MO: *last year of high school, you're going to different colleges...*

PEEP: *exactly. I want to let her know I value this relationship*

ME: *then you should*

MO: *I'm not saying it won't work, but long distance is messy*

Someone tapped on my door. Definitely not Granma; she had the habit of charging into my room without knocking or an announcement. Frida? Or Paul, my mind supplied. At this point, I was seeing more of him than I was Frida.

"Rasheed, I'm back," Frida said. "I brought everything we'll need. Are you ready?"

I sat up. "Uh, yeah, give me a minute!"

ME: *ttyl...gone to cook*

I hopped off the bed, body buzzing with excitement and nerves.

Frida and I hadn't spent time together since I was nine.

She'd taken me to an Animal Orphanage which had lots of colorful snakes and a hundred-year-old tortoise, and we'd gotten fried chicken afterwards. I remembered her smiling at how oily my face had gotten and me grinning at seeing her happy. It was one of the few good memories I had of her; the rest usually left me empty.

PEEP: *good luck, hope it turns out well*

Yeah, me too.

It'll be alright, I thought. I pocketed the phone, wiped my hands on my jeans, and marched to the kitchen.

We were quiet as we unpacked the ingredients.

I opened a bag of *sev*, took a handful, and munched it down.

"So, we'll start with peeling the potatoes. I think that's easier," Frida began. She opened the now neatly organized drawer and pulled out a potato peeler. Her eyes darted toward me and back to the potatoes. "Do you know its origins?"

"Not really." I grabbed half of the potatoes and began to peel.

Frida cleared her throat. "Uh, well the actual name is *Kachri bateta*. It's an Indian food, but we call it Babu Kachri after the Indian man who started selling it." She sounded like she was reading from a prompt.

If this set the tone for how the rest of the evening would go, then we'd be drowning in awkward before we even got halfway done.

"It's actually easy to make. It's pretty straightforward."

"Oh, nice."

There was a long but pleasant silence as we got the potatoes peeled and diced. Frida was faster at it than I was, so she helped with mine. The small gesture cracked open a part of me I had locked away, and all sorts of nagging questions that had always needed answers crept out.

Why do you never stay? surfaced to the top. God no, that was too heavy.

We needed something lighter to break the ice.

Like my father, maybe?

I didn't know anything about him. Granma, who was my source, had met him twice before he died. All she knew was he'd been part of the local port authority and had died in a road accident.

"Wash those." She pointed to the potatoes and grabbed a mango. "I'll be slicing this, then we'll make the curry."

I did as asked, going even as far as washing each piece on its own before I slid closer to Frida by the stove. Being this close to her, I could smell the lavender-scented detergent we used and noted the wrinkled skin at the corner of her eye. She said nothing, and at the moment, I was content watching her crush garlic into an oiled pan. She then threw in spices, the potatoes, a bit of the mango, and added water. "We'll let it boil for a few minutes."

Granma strutted into the kitchen in her pumps, covered in the scent of thick perfume. She laughed in delight as she struck a pose. "*Eh, mnanionaje?*" She turned. "How do I look?"

She wore a blue floral dress that went past her knees. It was tight around her middle, and her lips were a dull red.

"You look good," Frida said automatically.

Granma shifted her weight from her left to her right, prompting a laugh from Frida.

"Eh, Rasheed, say something." Granma waved at herself.

"Umm you look like you're going somewhere important. Where *are* you going?"

"Paul and I are going to dinner. He's coming up the driveway. Is the hair okay?" She patted her locs, cornrowed at the top.

I did my best to refrain from rolling my eyes. That explained why she'd been oddly quiet tonight, and the TV was turned off. "That's nice."

She met my eyes. "Is everything going well?"

"Yeah, I'm fine."

Paul was dressed in a bright red dress shirt that went well with his beige dress pants and—thank the heavens—no brown leather jacket. He held a large bouquet of colorful flowers that Granma cooed over.

Granma said goodbye, and I noticed the shine and excitement in her eyes. Paul let his hand settle on her elbow as he ushered her out.

"*Mjibambe*," Frida called after them.

Oh, dear God. I hoped the type of fun Frida meant was the PG kind. Anything else and my brain would fall out.

"Do you think Paul is nice?" I asked.

She grabbed a paper towel and began wiping down the counter. "Yeah, he's fine. He adores Rukia." Her face didn't match the statement, her lips pressed together and her face scrunched up.

"I guess so."

She handed me another half of sliced mango. "Grate this while I clear the dishes."

By dishes she meant the potato peelers, a large dish, and two cups. She was almost as bad as Mrs. King, Peep's mum, when it came to cleanliness.

"So you really like being clean, huh?"

Amusement lined her lips. "I do. One thing I miss when I'm away is being in charge of my own cleaning."

I frowned. One thing she missed, and it was not me.

She grabbed a bowl. "That mango will go here. We'll mix it with the coconut flakes, throw in salt, sugar, and a few spices, mostly turmeric—how do you feel about chili?"

"Love it. Would I be a Tawi otherwise?"

Her lips stretched into a real smile, the one only Granma could pull out, where her teeth would show. "Good point. Well, that's how we make the chutney. We'll serve it together, and that's about it."

Oh. That was depressingly fast. Here I was thinking this would be a great bonding moment. When she said she'd show me how to cook *Babu Kachri*, she meant just that. I didn't know any other time Frida and I would get this opportunity. I might wake up tomorrow and she'd be gone, job or no job—she'd demonstrated that before. I had to grab this opportunity while it was still there.

"So, umm, can you tell me more about my father?"

Frida's movements slowed. She focused intently on opening the bag of coconut flakes. "He worked at the ports," she said in a low tone as if the words were fragile and could break.

"I know that. But I want to know more. Like, how'd you meet?"

A pause. "At a wedding."

She didn't elaborate.

"What was he like?"

She studied me before she took the small bowl I'd grated the mango into and upturned it into the larger one. "He had the same curls as yours."

I put my hand to my hair; I ran my fingers through it. Now I'd never cut it for sure.

"Wash that hand. It better not touch the food," she scolded.

I quirked my lips. That was the most motherly she had sounded in a while. I went to the sink and washed my hands.

"What was his favorite color?"

She hesitated. "Blue, he liked blue. He wore a lot of crisp blue shirts."

"Really? I like blue. What else?"

"He loved *pweza*—you know what that is?"

I had to process it first. "Octopus?"

"Yeah, he liked it as a stew for *ugali* or with rice. He liked the beach."

Warmth engulfed me. I was a little like him, then.

"So, we got this apartment near the beach." Her voice wobbled. "I want you to check if the curry is done. We want the potatoes well cooked until they start crumbling."

I returned to the pot of curry, but my eyes were on her, fascinated with the information, not wanting to look away. "What else?"

"Uh…" She passed a finger over her brow. "He liked music, especially anything by Michael Jackson."

I nodded.

"How are the potatoes?" she prompted.

I poked the potatoes with the spoon; a few crumbled. "They're doing okay, I guess."

She peeked into the pot. "Yeah, they're okay. Better start smashing them now before all the water evaporates and they start sticking to the pot. Not too hard though; it's not mashed potatoes we're interested in."

"Okay." I started poking the potatoes. "So, uh, was he excited about me?"

Frida sighed, pinched the bridge of her nose, and squeezed her eyes shut. "Look, Rasheed...can we talk about this when I'm more ready?"

One day, Adam, Peep, and I were racing each other on our bikes. I'd won and waved my hands up in triumph. By a fit of bad luck, I lost control and fell, headfirst. I hit the ground so hard, the earth seemed to quake, and pain had shot through my head like someone was throwing bricks at it. When I sat up, I couldn't tell Adam from Peep, and my head had rung for hours. Frida's words echoed the pain of that day. Her words pounded hard at my skull.

"What?" I said in shock.

"It's hard to talk about him."

I blinked. I was unsure—like, I could shed my skin with how unsure I felt. The respect-your-elders philosophy Granma had drummed into me demanded I do as she asked, give her space.

Give her time.

She'd had eighteen years. For eighteen years, I have been waiting for her to come to me.

"Keep mashing and stirring," she instructed. "We want a thick gravy."

I flicked my eyes to the pot, the thick bubbling liquid an accurate mirror of the anger rising up my chest. "I don't care," I said quietly.

Frida's eyes widened. "What?"

Apologize, I heard Granma say.

No, my mind rebelled. I'd avoided confrontation, but not anymore. I ignored the prickle at the back of my neck and stood for my truth. "I said I don't care about the food. I want to know about my father. You think speaking about my dead father is hard. I've gone my whole life with my mother ignoring me. I have an asshole for a grandfather and no knowledge of my father. I'm tired of your excuses, Frida. You've had eighteen years to get yourself together but didn't."

The words came out drowned in grief, the sting of tears close behind. I was panting like I had been running.

I was not going to break in front of her.

I headed for the front door. I grabbed my bike, hopped on, and started pedaling. I didn't want to be in the house any longer. I needed to get away.

Frida had the nerve! She was in pain? *Her?*

My chest grew heavy, and my breath quickened, coming out in short loud bursts.

At least she'd known him. I didn't have memories of him. Hell, we could argue I didn't even have a mom. And to think I hoped us doing something together meant we would be laying some kind of foundation.

I pedaled faster down the street to keep the tears from falling. I refused to cry. I was *not* going to cry. Not because of Frida.

I circled our street three times until I got my breathing under control, but I wasn't ready to back home. I patted my pockets and sighed with relief when I touched the bulge of my phone. I pulled it out to call Mo or Peep, but found Adam's name at the top of the list. I chewed the insides of my cheeks, considering it. Fuck it.

ME: *coming over, that alright?*

The reply didn't come immediately. I stared at the phone wondering if maybe this was a mistake. I stared at the screen, willing him to say yes.

My phone buzzed.

ADAM: *sure*

ME: *in the playhouse?*

ADAM: *okay*

ME: *on my way*

Chapter Seventeen

I was exhausted by the time I made it to Adam's place. I'd pushed myself, going at my fastest speed, which had drained my energy and most of the anger. I wanted my brain overworked because then I wouldn't overthink and regret my reaction. It was valid. Frida might have been in pain, but answers to my questions were long overdue.

I pushed my bike through the backyard and saw the faint glow of the playhouse. Adam had said he'd be waiting inside. I deposited the bike and hastened my pace.

Adam was on his back, phone propped on his stomach, knees bent. He put the phone aside and sat up the moment I crawled inside and crouched next to him. "Hey."

"Hey."

Adam lifted a brown paper bag. "I brought stuff."

I pulled the blankets over my legs—they were warm from Adam's body and had a slight hint of his cologne—then reached for the bag and peered inside. A tub of vanilla ice cream and a jar of peanut butter with two spoons. I tried to smile but my mind wandered back to the food I'd left behind and Frida saying she wasn't ready. "This is awesome."

"You're welcome."

Vanilla ice cream and peanut butter had been a thing when we were kids. Natalie would give the biggest scoop to the best behaved, which was me. "Only thing missing is Peep and his bacon."

Adam pretended to gag. "Only Peep can find bacon and ice cream tasty."

"Peep could eat a wet sock and find it delicious."

Adam snorted. "Pass a spoon; I've been wanting to do this for a while."

We took a couple of bites in silence.

"What's it like having a dad?" I asked.

Adam narrowed his eyes at me. His skin seemed to glow in the low light. The sight took me back to the movies when his breath had brushed my skin and we'd been leaning toward each other.

"My dad specifically?"

"No, like in a general sense. If your dad wasn't there, what would life be like?"

"Knowing there's someone else I can count on." Adam worried his lower lip between his teeth. "My favorite memory of my dad was when mom was pregnant with the twins, and doctors were worried she might not make it. I was scared, you know, but Dad was there, doing everything he could to cheer me up and make sure I was alright. It's fucked to admit, but all I thought about was—if mom died, Dad would be there, and that made me feel safe."

I smiled.

"I like the way he stands up for us, and himself, and he gives good advice once he's had two glasses of wine, you know, once he relaxes."

I snorted at the idea of a tipsy Mr. Herman.

"Do you know your dad?"

"No. He died before I was born."

"I'm sorry."

I've never missed him because I didn't know him. I didn't know how to react to that. Should I be angry at the missed opportunity, or simply shrug it off because he was dead, and it wouldn't change anything?

"Is that what's got you upset?"

"It's my mom."

"Oh, what did she do?"

Nothing and everything at the same time. I huffed and shoved a spoonful of the ice cream into my mouth. "I don't think she cares much about me."

Adam's lips pinched together. "What? That's…"

"I wish I was being a brat about this." It would hurt less. "Today was the first time in forever we spent time together—and I mean since I was probably nine—and it turned into a fucking disaster."

Adam reached out his hand and squeezed my bicep. "Sorry she doesn't see how amazing a son she has."

Embarrassment washed over me, and a laugh burst out. "Oh my God, now I'm thinking of every bad thing I've done."

"Well, I mean, duh. You're a teenager. We're the bane of existence. The reason the world is going to shit."

"Damn, okay."

"I only mean parents are obligated to give support and guidance. That's their job, whether you're an angel or Satan's spawn—okay, the Satan's Spawn is debatable...though you could argue bad parenting?"

"Yup, look at every villain origin story ever."

"And what else would they do with us anyway?"

"Use us for free labor?"

Adam snorted.

"Do you want a hug?"

I shrugged. "I mean, if you insist."

"I insist, I'm great with hugs."

We stared at each other. "I think one of us needs to move," Adam finally said.

"Yeah, not me though. I'm the victim."

"Fine."

Adam put the ice cream and peanut butter aside and pushed himself closer to me. His head knocked with mine, and we groaned.

"You seriously are hardheaded," I said rubbing my forehead.

"Shut up." He placed his hand on my shoulder, hauled me to him, and wrapped his arms tightly around me.

I froze, startled, unsure of what to do. We'd never been this close before. I lifted my arms and circled them around his back, then did the one thing I'd wanted to do in forever—burrowed my head in his neck. My nose brushed against his skin as his warmth wrapped itself around me.

"I'm sorry your mom hasn't been around to see she's got herself a great son."

He had a point. I wasn't evil. I was good in school. I did my homework on time. I did well on tests. I didn't torment adults or my peers. I helped old women with their gardens. Sure, sometimes I conveniently forgot to do my chores and sometimes skipped a class or two.

Why couldn't she be nice to me, at the least?

My gut clenched in despair. I pressed harder onto Adam. I shut my eyes and forced my thoughts somewhere else. Somewhere where I didn't hurt.

After a while, Adam's hand slid lower and landed on the small of my back. He started to rub in a soothing motion, his fingers touching a patch of skin where my shirt had ridden up. I became more aware of him and me plastered to him. Our upper bodies were very much touching, but my legs were cramping up from the weird angle they were in.

"What's your Granma said about it?"

"Nothing."

"Nothing?"

"We've never discussed it."

Adam's hand pressed down. His other squeezed my arm. "I'm sorry."

I brought my head up and found my eyes were exactly on the same level as his. I cringed at his pitying look. "No puppy-dog look."

"I can't help it... It's hard to imagine."

I pulled back, ready to abandon the comfort of his arms, but he held on tight.

"I will wipe the expression off." He shook his head and smiled. "See."

"Good, the last thing I want from Adam Herman is pity," I said honestly.

Adam smiled. "What's the first?"

My eyes flickered to those lips. I averted my gaze and found a poster of a smiling girl with glowing hands. The way the dim light fell over half her face made it seem like she was watching me with a sinister expression. "Um, I guess your denim jackets. I like those."

The brightness in Adam's expression seemed to dull, but he managed a grin. "All you had to do was ask."

He finally let go. I lay down and pulled the blankets over me, and immediately, the sleep started to creep in. Adam fell back and lay on his side, watching me.

"Umm, are you trying to weird me out?" I asked after several seconds of his stare still fixed on me.

"No...do you think there's a way to fix your relationship with your mom?"

I shrugged. "I don't think it's up to me anymore."

"Would you forgive her?"

I clutched the blanket tighter. I thought back to Frida grinning at me. It wouldn't hurt to have her in my life—okay, it did hurt to have her in my life...but if she cared, then it would be nice. Having Granma was great, but we were *two*, and that had been very evident when she was taken to hospital and I had no one to lean on. No one to grieve with. "She'd have to mean it."

"Yeah."

I yawned and closed my eyes.

"I'm thinking I'll do it," Adam announced after what felt like forever, when sleep was about to sink its teeth firmly in me.

"Hmm?"

"Come out to my family."

It took a moment for my mind to register the words. I opened my eyes.

"I've been going back and forth with it, and you know what—I'll do it...for real."

"OhmyGod that's huge. Are you sure?"

He groaned. "I mean, I guess so... I can't stop thinking about it. When I..." He glanced at me, then at the roof. "Well, when I look at a guy and think he's attractive, I kind of feel like I'm hiding something. Only, my dad might be an ass about it."

"He doesn't have to know."

"I know; exactly why I've been going back and forth with it. But there's no telling one person something in my family, everyone ends up finding out. They seriously don't know how to keep their mouths zipped. They're always one innuendo away from spilling the beans. Seriously, rejoice you don't have three older brothers or younger twin sisters."

"Okay, out of context it sounds horrific."

"The experience is worse."

"I'm pretty sure they'd be supportive."

"Yeah, they're, like, twenty percent okay."

I laughed. Throwing caution to the wind, I asked, "Is there a cute guy?"

Adam went still. "Umm."

My stomach clenched. "So that's a yes?"

He thought about it. "Okay, I can't say this today." He covered his eyes with his hands.

I moved closer to him. "You've gotta say it now." I had to know...because I was a sucker for pain.

Kris? It had to be him. He had a bright smile. How did you not like someone with a bright smile and carefully arranged teeth?

Pain pricked my chest. No. It was fine, I tried to convince myself. If he liked Kris, then I'd be spared crushing on him for months.

"Promise not to laugh."

Oh, Adam, I'll probably be sobbing. "I'll do my best."

"You'll laugh; promise you won't laugh."

"Will pinky swearing make it better?"

He uncovered his face and turned to me. "No. How about you'll owe me."

"What?"

"Anything I want at any time."

"Not that I'll be laughing."

"But if you do laugh?"

"Yes, I'll owe you," I huffed. "Now say it already."

"Hmm..." His stare bounced from me to the walls of the playhouse. "I don't know where to start."

I smiled. "I think you're sweating a little." I let my finger trail his forehead, and it was moist.

"'Cause you're steaming up my face."

"Do you know how fun seeing you this nervous is? Now please say it. Please, or I'll stuff my unwashed socks in your mouth."

"Okay, okay," he groaned. "I think I had a crush on you back then."

He had to be joking. A cruel joke. I started howling in laughter.

"You promised." Adam's face was blurry. Tears clouded my eyes.

"Sorry." It was so funny. Adam had had a crush on me. I wanted to ring his neck. Did he know how much self-doubt he had fostered? Now he was telling me the way he'd touched me meant something. I rolled away before he could clamp his hand over my mouth.

Adam managed to pin my hands over my head and sit on my stomach to keep me still. "What the fuck is so funny? You promised." Adam's lips twisted in irritation.

"I know," I breathed. "I'm sorry."

"You owe me now."

My phone vibrated. It could wait. Adam's grip loosened, and he got off me.

He'd had a crush on *me*! Happiness filled my heart. I grinned at him.

"You liked me?"

"Yeah." Adam scowled. "It's not funny."

"I know, sorry. It's..." I swallowed. Could I tell him? If I did, I'd have to explain the real reason why we'd stopped being friends for a while. I didn't have it in me. It would be pretty humiliating. But if he'd liked me back then...

"You dated Sarah," I pointed out.

"I was confused about what I felt. I thought—I thought I liked you as a friend."

I studied him. His eyes were troubled.

My phone started to vibrate. I groaned when I saw Granma's texts.

> GRANMA: *Frida says you left, at night, without telling her where you're going...*
>
> GRANMA: *where are you?*

Chapter Eighteen

Granma stubbed the air with her index finger. "I do not like you being out late at night. You're grown enough to know this. How many times do I have to say it?"

"Once is enough," I said in a solemn tone, then contorted my face into a sorrowful expression that would hopefully make Granma end her lecture.

She deepened her glower, unimpressed. "Why would you leave? I left you cooking." She motioned to the kitchen then to Frida, who sat still as a rock on the sofa watching us.

I ground my teeth to avoid glancing at her. In my mind, Frida was not in the same room as me. She was hopping on a spaceship to go back to wherever. It was not an easy task with my heart still sore from her words, but it had to be done.

"What happened?" Granma asked.

Frida hadn't told her, then. Why would I expect her too? I would have to be the one to make Granma aware. But how was she not aware of the cracks between Frida and me? Would she understand? How would she react? Could I do it with Frida seated there?

I cracked a knuckle. God, I couldn't do it now while I felt raw and unbalanced.

"I was—I won't do it again."

"Don't," she warned.

"Yes," I said quickly, happy she was winding down. "Uh. How was your—your date?" I was eager to steer the conversation in a new direction before she decided to berate me about my other faults. When was the last time I cleaned my room?

"It would have been perfect if you had behaved."

"I'm sorry."

Her forehead smoothed out. "I had a good time. I ate the most delicious fudge cake. I'm tempted to try baking one.

"You should."

"You won't get a piece if you're difficult."

I blew out air.

*

Frida pretended the confrontation had not happened and went out of her way to start conversations about everything unimportant—what did I care about wooden spoons compared to plastic ones? She was only embarrassing herself, and I was too annoyed at her audacity to ignore what had happened.

I didn't want to spend time at home anymore. I tagged along with Mo as he shopped for books and spent time at the Hermans, Adam's earlier confession burning in my mind. We were never alone though. Sometimes Eric was there, too, barely uttering a word, and if he did, it came out mumbled. He and Adam would do some coding or play video games. I didn't mind as, occasionally, Adam would look over and smile, or if he was passing by, he'd squeeze my shoulder, which made it hard to concentrate on my homework. When I didn't have schoolwork, the twins would rope me into doing stuff with them. It was why I had flaking black nail polish on my toes.

Today, they had managed to convince me to come over so they could try finger curls on my hair. It was either that or spend my Wednesday afternoon at home alone, unable to avoid thinking about Frida.

The kids coated my hair with a lot of conditioner and started the process. It had been a while since someone had messed with my hair. I'd forgotten how relaxing it could be to have fingers poking and prodding, and their chatter soothed me.

"Boo!" Em whispered in my ear, making me jump and causing them to giggle.

"What are you thinking about?" Maya asked. She wiped her foamy hands on a green towel.

Oh, we were done.

"Probably Adi," Em said.

"I'm not thinking about Adam," I said quickly.

"Then what?"

I huffed. "My mom."

"What'd she do?" Maya asked.

"Exist."

Emily snorted and handed me the mirror. I gasped in shock. I looked good. I laughed and went to touch it.

"Don't, you'll ruin it."

"Okay. I look like I belong in a music video." I turned left then right, stuck out my pinched lips and pretended to strike a pose.

"Yeah, but not with those clothes," Em said.

I frowned. I wore black jeans and a bright-yellow sweater shirt. "This is one of my best outfits." I'd spent longer than usual on my clothes, which was all I needed to know that I was trying to impress Adam. I knew how Sarah dressed, and she didn't come to play—designer jeans, makeup done on point, and a professional hairstyle. There was a niggling under my skin, wondering if I'd ever measure up.

Em shook her head at me in a clear sign of pity. I stuck out my tongue at her.

"Mom can be annoying too," Maya said.

"The worst." Em nodded. "She won't allow us to go to sleepovers." She fell on her bed with a heavy sigh. They didn't share a bedroom; Maya had taken Wally and Leo's old room, while Emily had remained in their old room, painted it a pale pink, and stuck posters of K-pop bands on her walls.

"Ever."

"We usually miss all the gossip and secrets."

"Sorry guys." To be young and nine. At that age, I still thought Frida cared. The toys she would send, happy she thought about me, cared about me. Now, I'm sure she'd done it out of obligation, or she'd gotten tired along the way.

"What did your mom do?" Maya asked.

"She..." I paused, unsure how to explain it in a way she would understand. "She didn't give me—" Motherly love, love, affection, support is what came to mind, but I settled for "Bacon."

Maya's eyebrows pinched together the same way Adam's did. "Bacon?"

"Yes. I really wanted bacon." I bobbled my head. "But she doesn't like, uh, sharing the bacon. She kept it to herself even though it was clear I was starving for it."

"That's so mean," Maya said.

"If someone refused to share their bacon, I'd make sure to put snails in their shoes."

"Or spiders."

"Or spiders!" Em sat up, excited at where the conversation was going. "Or let loose a big snake in the bathroom while they're in there."

Maya grinned and joined her sister. "They'd be stuck between finishing their business, or calling for help."

I giggled nervously. "Okay, guys, don't get carried away."

Em pouted. "We were just getting started."

"We haven't gotten to knives yet."

I laughed. "You weirdos, and I mean that in a nice way."

There was a knock on the door. I went to open it. Adam stood on the other side. His eyes widened before his expression softened. "Hey." His voice was like an electric current down my spine, jolting me awake.

I stood straighter, met his eyes, and said in a hoarse whisper, "Hey."

He smelled as if he'd fallen in an energy drink, but my focus was on how his lips had Chapstick on them and fighting the urge to lean down and taste the flavor.

I didn't realize we were standing there awkwardly until Emily appeared and asked, "You going to stand there all day?"

That made heat rise up my cheeks. "No," I said to her, then to Adam, "You coming in?"

"Yeah." He took a tentative step inside, glanced at his sisters, then back at me. "I thought I heard you laughing, but was, like, what would Rasheed be doing here?"

"Getting my hair done." I pointed to my head. "What do you think?"

"You look good," he said earnestly.

My confidence flared. "Thanks."

Adam joined us but went crazy when we suggested we give him a hair makeover—no one got to touch his hair.

*

"Are you staring at my ass?" Adam was scraping a pot. His mouth twisted in a smirk.

I blanched, embarrassed at being caught so red-handed. He wore thin sweats that molded around his peachy butt—it couldn't be helped that my eyes were pulled there. "No, I'm not." I cleared my throat. "But I want you to know, it was wiggling."

"You're an idiot."

I laughed.

"Remember when I said you owed me?"

"Umm, no?"

"Try again. I'm cashing in now. You're going to help me with the dishes." The Hermans had had a heavy meal, and they'd left a stack of dishes, most of them greasy.

"Umm, can I say no?"

"Nope. Come on; it's all set up for you." He patted the sink affectionately. I groaned. "And to top it off, I'll play Mongolian metal so your ears can bleed."

"Doubt it could be worse than your British accent," I mumbled.

Adam paused, clasped his hands, and cocked his head. "Did you...insult me?"

"Sorry?" My lips twitched.

"This means war, Rasheed. War."

"Ah, I'm bigger than you."

"But I'm stronger."

"I'm taller."

"By half a head. Here." He threw a white tablecloth. "A white flag. Wave it and say you'll owe me, or I'll have no option but to embarrass you."

The challenge in his voice was hot. I thrummed with excitement and did the only logical thing. I threw the towel at him, palmed some soap suds from the sink, and rushed to slather his face with them. Adam got a glint in his eye, accompanied by a wolfish grin. It was all the warning I got before a war ensued.

After a minute or two of struggling, he pinned me against the counter, its edge biting into my ass as Adam tried to put the suds in my mouth. He'd won so far, getting me in my eyes and ears, and I'd barely touched him— turns out Adam lifting weights was not an aesthetic. I gripped his right wrist to keep the foam from my mouth as his other hand was tight against my waist, and I held on to his left bicep.

I was so going to end up with foam in my mouth, and a Mt. Kilimanjaro-sized bulge on its way to becoming an Everest pressed against Adam, which sounded good and all in my dreams, but the reality of it was scary.

"Say ahh," Adam singsonged, and his breath washed over me as he leaned closer, nearly overpowering me. Okay, so I'd end up with the foam in my mouth—ew—but I had to do something about keeping Adam from feeling my erection.

I maneuvered my right hand from his bicep to his waist so I could keep his lower section a safe distance, but my plan was thwarted when Adam managed to completely overpower me and lather my mouth with soapy foam.

Adam laughed. "We need a Santa; Christmas is around the corner." I dropped my hand from his waist, thinking the imminent danger was averted. But then Adam—the bastard—leaned in, pushing himself closer to reach for the sink behind me, for more foam, and my very own Kilimanjaro rubbed against his thigh.

We both froze.

This was torture, and I was going to die from either lack of air or my insides melting from the heat enveloping me. I was vibrating with the need to close the distance between us and have his lips pressed to mine.

Adam's hands tightened, and he swayed closer. We were eye to eye now, the smell of tomato sauce we'd had for dinner on his breath and the lemon scent of soap on his shirt. Adam went a step further and pressed a chaste kiss on my lips that turned me into a puddle. I held on tight, which seemed to encourage Adam. He leaned in for a kiss, and I opened my mouth to welcome him.

The kiss made me heady, and the world around me went hazy. He tasted sweet, and I couldn't get enough. His hands wandered up my back, cupped my cheeks, and found their way into my hair. I shuddered and dug my fingernails into his back. He made a soft sound, muffled by our lips pressed together. I wanted to hear it again and again.

Please, brain, I hope you're taking notes so I never forget this.

Unease doused the pooling heat. What if this strained the new friendship Adam and I had? What if I ruined it?

Mr. Herman coughing in the next room was all the sign I needed. Holding on to the remnants of self-control, I stepped out of Adam's reach to give us both some breathing space. Somehow, Adam looked turned on, confused, disappointed, embarrassed, and a bit freaked out all at once.

"M-maybe..." I started breathlessly. We were both panting softly. "Maybe we should close other tabs before opening this one."

"Now I know, Adam, you were not playing with the water!" Natalie barked from the entry of the kitchen. "And you, too, Rasheed? Aren't you both a little too grown for this?"

Adam's eyes went wide. Shit, we'd completely forgotten there were other people in the house. A minute or two sooner and she'd have walked in on us, and there was no telling what kind of shitstorm would have formed.

"Sorry, Ma, I'll clean it up," Adam said, sounding spooked.

I cleared my throat. "Sorry, we'll clean it up."

"You better." Natalie shot us glares at the mess we'd made. Even the dishes that sat on the drying rack were now soapy. We cleaned up the mess in excruciating silence. It didn't help that Natalie stayed in the kitchen talking on the phone, and every once in a while, when one of us caught her eyes, she glared.

My clothes were stuck on me, glued by my nervous sweat despite the coolness of the house. Even with Frida, I didn't have this much of an urge to dissolve into the air and disappear. I tried to convince myself Adam likely needed to process. It was his first time with a dude after all.

Soon as I was done, I got the hell out of there. Too scared to stay and discuss what had happened. I reasoned it was to give Adam space too—okay, it was just easier.

Oh my God. I was such a coward.

Chapter Nineteen

"What's with you?" Mo asked. He handed me a paper. Mo and I were helping Peep with Tani's DIY gift, a book that would detail their relationship highlighted in pictures and with Peep's doodles for occasions where there were none. Mo had given himself the leadership role because he had the keenest eye for design and was a perfectionist. Normally, I would have sooner spooned my eye out than do DYI stuff—I'd already gotten two paper cuts—but staying home while Frida was there didn't appeal, and the Herman house was out of the question since that kiss happened.

Ohemgee. That kiss. Those lips, soft like marshmallows and as sweet.

But the thing that was really nagging at me was Frida. I was still in shock by her gall to say she needed more space. Thinking about it made my blood boil. I wanted an explanation and an apology.

Mo slapped me with a sheet of paper. "What?"

I sighed. "There's a lot going on."

"What a lot?" Peep asked. He was on his phone religiously texting Tani. I wanted what they had, not casual stuff.

"Can you please help? We're doing this for you." Mo pointed to the work on the table.

"Sorry, in a minute," said Peep, eyes fixed on his phone.

"We need this done today." Mo sounded frankly agitated. "I've got a date with Malia tomorrow, and we can't get much done if you'll do nothing but text, and you—" Mo jabbed his finger in my face. "—need to concentrate."

"Alright, alright." Peep huffed, put his phone down, and stared at the mess we'd made. "Why did I think this was a good idea? It's too much work."

"It's worth it."

"Plus, you can't quit now," Mo said. "We're almost done with junior prom, and then we'll only have summer left."

Peep groaned. "I should have put together a video collage with a love song playing instead. This is a waste of paper. And what if she thinks it's stupid?"

"She won't," Mo assured him. He waved at the half-finished book. "Look at the detail."

It did look decent. The pictures, Peep's doodles, my hand-lettering, and the way Mo had put it all together. It was cute.

"Listen to Mo, Peep. Look how pretty he made it." He'd even thought to put in astrology Easter eggs and use Tani's favorite colors, pink and yellow.

Peep smiled. "You're right. I didn't know you were good at this."

"I know, I'm talented. I keep saying it. Now, let's do this." Mo pointed the scissors at me. "And don't you dare lose focus."

We worked in silence for a few minutes before Peep blurted out, "What a lot?"

"I'm thinking—" I fixed my eyes on a picture of Peep and Mo at a music festival, Tani hugging Peep from behind. I liked how they were complements of each other—Peep had on his usual black outfit, and Tani was in rainbow colors, her hair in pink-and-blue braids.

"Work and talk," Mo said.

Peep nodded. "Did she apologize?"

I groaned. "Nope, I doubt she will. She's gone back to life as if nothing happened. Except now she's acting a bit perky, and it's driving me crazy."

"Your mom needs to take charge and stop being an ass," Mo said without filters.

"Ah, thanks."

"He has a point."

"I've also been thinking; I should apologize to Scott, you know?" Yesterday, I walked into a guy's elbow raised in hi five because I thought I saw Scott. It had been a false alarm. "It's not fair I expect Frida to apologize for being an ass, and I haven't apologized to Scott."

"Dude, I don't think you can really compare the two. One is your mother, the other you'll forget in, like, a year or two."

"Not that what you did to Scott is right, but they're two different things."

From a distance, they could be identical—and if I'm being honest, Frida refusing to show emotion was expected. It was her nature. She didn't mislead me. If anything, at least she was honest, even if it was misplaced. But what I'd done to Scott was plain mean. I'd led him on and failed to deliver.

"I'll do it; I'll apologize to Scott," I said resolutely.

"We need to see it." Mo narrowed his eyes on my hands, currently stalling, and then back at me. I rolled my eyes and continued cutting.

"Yeah, you've been saying that on and off."

"I mean it this time."

"Of course you do," Mo said.

"I don't like that tone."

"Oh my." We turned to see Mrs. King standing there with a horrified expression. "Abiloye Peter King," she squealed—Peep's full name.

He groaned. "Ma, we'll clean it, promise."

Her eyes roamed the mahogany table, cluttered with markers, papers, and other stuff, then the fancy carpet now littered with paper. She pressed her lips in clear distaste. "You're not even using a coaster, and there's crumbs everywhere!"

Peep glared at us, and I did the dutiful thing by placing my can of coke on a coaster. That did not seem to appease her.

"Sorry, Mrs. King," Mo and I said at the same time.

"We'll clean up," Peep promised.

Interior design was Mrs. King's passion, which meant she had chosen her furniture carefully. On top of that, she was also a fan of antiseptics and bleach. She would clean every floor because juice spilled in the kitchen.

Coming here was usually a last resort; we couldn't go to our house because I didn't want to be around Frida until I got an apology—not that I was holding my breath. Mo's place was out too. His older asshole of a brother and his friends were there, and unless you found toxic environments conducive, the most reasonable thing was to steer clear.

"The right way?"

"Yes, the right way."

The "right way" meant using a bunch of various disinfectants and too much time.

"Okay." She exhaled, mumbling something under her breath. "Are you hungry?"

"We ate."

"And you cleaned the plates?"

"We were going to do that."

"Abiloye."

"Mom," Peep whined.

"Okay." The wrinkle on her forehead smoothed out, and with a final nod, she left the room.

"Thanks guys; now we have to *clean*." Peep turned and glared at Mo and me.

"Next time let's not do this," Mo said diplomatically. "Maybe buy her a cactus or something."

We glued the remaining photos, I finished the hand lettering, and we decided Peep could do the doodles on his own. Then it was Peep's turn to take charge and direct the cleaning, making sure we didn't do it half-assed.

"Guys, it occurred to me this might be our last year together."

The words made my heart ache. We'd be spread around the country. Peep had applied mostly to schools on the East Coast, Mo on the West Coast—the farthest he could get from his family without leaving the country—and me, I'd be in the Midwest if life was kind to me.

I sniffled. Mo and Peep exchanged startled glances.

"Are you crying?"

"No." I sniffed and then focused on wiping down the table. "Something in my eye."

The silence made my skin crawl. I'd cried in front of Peep twice—when he broke his arm and when Adam started dating Sarah. He'd cried in front of me zero times. I cleared my throat, ready to set the conversation on a new plane. "I meant it; I want to apologize to Scott."

"You should," Peep said.

"I will."

"Do it tomorrow," Mo said.

"Tomorrow as in tomorrow?" My eyebrows shot up.

"Yes, tomorrow, and if you don't, never ever bring him up again. Ever. If you do, you'll have to buy us a meal of our choosing," Peep said.

"You've been talking about him for, like, forever. It's time to act bro. If you don't, you're buying us lunch, and I am thinking something fancy. A place that requires a tie."

"Now hold on. I am not buying anyone lunch."

"You won't have to if you actually do it," Peep pointed out.

"But he blocked me on every platform."

Mo pointed out, "You can apologize face-to-face."

"What?" I shrieked. "No." I shook my head adamantly. It sounded impossible. "And you want me to do it tomorrow?"

"Yes."

"But it's Sunday."

"I'm hearing a lot of excuses. You know where he lives; go and apologize."

I glared at Peep. "I tutor the Herman twins."

"How'd that even happen; you're not a professional."

"I know. It's for *fun*, and I get to use their very clean pool."

"Is that the only thing you do there?" Peep smirked.

My cheeks warmed. I hadn't told them about Adam and I making out. I wasn't sure if his sexuality was meant to be a tightlipped secret or not, and I didn't want to risk telling it if he was not ready to be out. More signs that the best way to move forward was to have a conversation about it, but of course, that wasn't how I worked. The painful part was realizing it didn't make me that different from Frida. Really, same face on different sides of a coin.

I really had to apologize to Scott.

"Fine. I'll cancel." I put down the can and cloth I'd been using and dug into my pocket to pull out my phone. I brought up Em and Maya's shared contact.

"This is so hard," I said.

Peep raised an eyebrow. "You've not even done anything."

"I'm thinking buying us a meal can be a kind of closure on its own."

A knot formed in my gut. Tomorrow or never. Time I faced my mistakes. Time I buried this.

"Okay," I said slowly, then louder. "Okay, I'll do it."

"Tomorrow."

"Yes, tomorrow."

I typed the message. *Won't make it tomorrow, something I gotta do.*

"Tomorrow, then." The knot tightened.

I didn't have to do this, a voice reasoned.

I did and I would. I had to be better than Frida, and that meant going head-to-head with my mistakes.

I put the phone away and checked that the vase, which acted as the center piece, was indeed dead center "How would I start?"

"By saying sorry."

*

Scott and I met in the drama club at the end of last year when Peep volunteered us to help paint the winter play sets. First time I saw him, he had his fingers running through his thick Harry Styles–type hair, back when he was starting out.

I'd seen him in school before and labeled him as attractive and unattainable (every crush starts out in those two boxes), but seeing him up close had blown me away. I'd stared until he gave me a quizzical look, probably wondering who the creep was. He caught me more than once stealing glances, and one day, he smiled. A few days later, he approached me. And then, we were a thing, but of course, I ruined it when the attraction started to bloom into something more and sent me running.

One day, everything was good, the next, anxiety was ringing my neck, whispering in my ear in a seductive and assuring tone, *this won't last, jump ship before he wrecks you.* And I had. Then, like the end of an eighties rock song, the relationship had faded to nothing. We'd never even talked about it being over; it had just been over.

The thing that haunted me was the hopeful expression on his face when I'd seen him after all the shit I'd done. He'd wanted me to ask him to stay and wanted me to fight for him, but I'd let him go.

I was an asshole.

My determination started to chip away once I was on his street, his blue Ford parked in the driveway. Shit. I groaned. I was really going to do this. My nerves made it impossible to cycle. I stopped and tried to relax.

Help me, I cant do it! I sent the text. I really didn't think I could do it. Was there a point?

I clenched my fingers around the phone. All I needed to do was cover the remaining distance, get to their front door, knock on the door, and apologize. Oh fuck, it even sounded complicated in my head.

PEEP: *Yes you can, just knock on the door and say sorry. You don't need a whole speech or anything.*

"Yes, I can," I repeated to myself.

MO: *no shame in turning back, we can go to Polly's and you can buy me donuts*

I shuffled my feet. The house, a wide one-story with peeling white paint stood, imposing, before me. I didn't have to do it.

PEEP: *don't listen to him*

I breathed out.

Frida—how much easier my life would have been if she had apologized.

Fuck it. I pocketed the phone and pushed the bicycle the rest of the way. He hated me. There was nothing to lose.

I rang the bell, a dog started to bark, someone cussed, and heavy boots clumped toward me. I held my breath. Shit, this was it. I was going to faint. I should have stayed home. Was it too late to head back?

The door jerked open. A woman with unsettling blue eyes and piercings on her nostrils glared at me impatiently. This had to be Ana, the sister who was a singer. We'd never met. If I'd stayed with Scott another week, when her tour ended, we would have then. "Yes?"

"Uh. Hey, umm, is Scott around?"

Ana gave me a once over before she narrowed her eyes. "Who are you?"

"Rasheed."

"He know you're coming?"

"No... But it's important."

Ana shrugged. "Wait here, then." She shut the door in my face. I shifted the weight on my feet and wiped my sweaty palms on my jeans.

I still had time to get the hell out of here. But leaving now would be even more of an ass move.

Scott opened the door, poked his head out, and let his jaw drop when he saw me standing on their porch. "The fuck are you doing here?"

My heart started pounding. My knees wobbled.

"Okay. Uh." Where to start? I'd rehearsed a speech last night, written it down in my notes app and everything. There was a whole monologue. The contents evaporated.

"That doesn't mean you answer, asshole. It means you leave." Scott's glare intensified.

"I came to apologize."

Scott snorted. "Really?"

"Yeah."

"We're not getting back together, ever," Scott said in finality. "I'd rather chew cheap hairy lipstick every day for the rest of my life."

"I know. I, uh, came here to apologize," I said again quickly. Scott folded his arms, but didn't say a word. I exhaled. "I'm sorry I was an ass to you. I'm sorry I ghosted you, I'm sorry I pulled away from you without any logical explanation." I rubbed my eyes. "I thought—I thought it was becoming serious, and it scared me. I wanted to say sorry. I'm sorry; you didn't deserve any of that."

Scott was quiet for a while. He studied me for a long time, and I fiddled with my hands. He looked gorgeous. He'd done something with his face to highlight his blue eyes, applied a light-pink blush.

"You were a dick, to be clear. And the dodging, that was pathetic as fuck."

"Yeah." I hunched my shoulders.

Scott glanced away refusing to meet my eyes now. The silence was cutting, each second made the guilt dig deeper. I could run away.

"Look," Scott said. I shifted my focus from his blue Vans and my discolored tennis shoes to him. "It hurt what you did. I didn't understand it. If you didn't love me back, you didn't have to say it. Why did you erase me from your life?"

I rubbed a hand behind my neck. "I panicked. It doesn't excuse it, of course. I got scared and made a stupid decision. By the time I realized I was being stupid, I didn't know how to take it back."

Scott's frown deepened. "You got issues."

I laughed. "I do."

He shook his head and sighed. "I'm sorry I broke your pen. That was bad behavior. I don't forgive you. But I'll definitely try to forget you."

"Okay," I said in a small voice.

I pocketed my hands. Bounced my gaze from the wall to him. "So, umm, how have you been?"

Scott cocked his head and arched an eyebrow. "I'm not going to tell you I'm doing good so you can be relieved, but I'm not doing bad either."

"Yeah, I get it."

"Anyway, your time's up. Bye, Rasheed." He started for the door. I felt an urge to beg him to forgive me, but I had to hold on to some self-respect.

"Bye, Scott."

I walked to my bike feeling hollow—but a good kind. The kind that said I'd emptied out some old things and created space for new.

Chapter Twenty

PEEP: *did Mo send you an SOS?*

> ME: *he did. I asked him what's up and he hasn't replied*

> PEEP: *you're the worst! He could be dying!*

> ME: *last time he sent one was because his green and blue jacket was missing...*

> PEEP: *I think it's serious, check out his posts.*

The post was a meme of a cartoon character lying in a pool of tears. The next few posts were much the same, quotes about how pain was insufferable. The most shocking and out of place thing was seeing he had posted one of Tani's poems: *I can't take this pain, circulating through my vein. It's as bitter as poison, how can I explain?*

Okay, Tani had to have better poems than that. I was grateful she didn't do spoken word and Peep didn't have to drag us to her shows—I'd die.

> ME: *is he alright? What happened?*

PEEP: *I don't know the details. Want to go check on him? he's not picking up*

ME: *now?*

PEEP: *yes, now. Last one there gets to hold him while he cries*

ME: *I have a bike*

Granma was in front of the TV as I rushed to put on my jacket and shoes. Paul wasn't here. He'd finally remembered he had to make a living and was finishing up on the resin and wood vases he'd been commissioned to make. Frida was home, too, her eyes focused on her laptop and a set of notebooks next to her. She didn't look up. Didn't acknowledge me.

"And where are you going?" Granma asked.

"To see Mo. I think something happened."

Her eyebrows knitted. "Is everything okay?"

"I'm not sure."

She tilted her head to the side. "I never see you anymore. *Kweni unahama na sijui?*"

"If I moved out, where would I go?"

She shrugged. "You are the one to tell me. Where have you been? You've been missing the show." She pointed to the TV.

"I know."

"There was a scene where Derek was without a shirt." Her lips twitched. "That's the reason you watch it?"

"Oh my God, Granma, stop." I palmed my face.

"*Nimedanganya?* Have I lied?"

"No, you haven't." I nodded to the door. "Can I go?"

"And don't be late."

Peep got to Mo's place before I did; he sat on the hood of his car, swiping through his phone. I was sweaty and already starting to stink, the only positive was I did have on a dark shirt and dark jeans and a black nylon bomber jacket.

"You should really learn to drive man." Peep grinned and pocketed his phone.

"One day." I made a show of looking around. "You forget your arm?"

He pocketed the phone. "No, Tani has her own stuff."

"Interesting. See, I thought you carried the hands and her the legs."

He shrugged. "Let's do this."

*

"What the hell!" Peep exclaimed when we stepped into Mo's room.

It was in disarray and more chaotic than usual. There were books everywhere: on the bed, the desk, the dresser, and piled into small towers on the floor.

Mo ignored him and waved at the neatly arranged shelf behind him that covered the entire wall. "What do you think?"

"Umm, it's not overflowing?" I said.

It was the only thing in the room that was in order—a first. His room was so poorly maintained and cluttered that Mo had found several dead roaches once.

"Exactly." He ran his fingers over the spines with a smirk.

"But where will the others go?" Peep asked as his gaze swept the room.

"In there." Mo pointed to a box beside the dresser.

"It says 'donations,'" Peep said.

"I'm giving them away."

"Okay, maybe he's dying," I mumbled, low enough only Peep could hear.

"Hold on." Peep held up a hand. "You're giving your books away?"

"Yeah."

"And no one is forcing you?" Peep squinted at Mo.

"Blink twice if you're under duress," I said.

"What? No. They need to go." He reached for a pair of box sets lying on his bed and tugged them into the box. Normally, at this point, Mo would be squealing in distress at the prospect of being separated from any of his books.

"I mean, it's a great idea but are you sure?" I asked. "You're always on about how each book is like a memory bank and how they form a roadmap of the life you've lived."

Mo hesitated. "I'm sure."

"Why the SOS then?" Peep asked.

"The fourth row fell, and everything came crashing down. Dad screwed it back on."

Peep pinched the bridge of his nose. "You could have told us that over text if you answered our texts and calls."

Mo searched under some books for his phone. He looked at the screen and chuckled nervously. "My bad. To be fair, I was sorting through this mess."

I groaned. "Dude, I could be doing homework."

More truthfully, I could have been stalking Adam online for clues on what he thought about us making out. I'd decided "making out" was the most accurate term because there'd been tongue, a press of bodies, and we'd both been turned on. Thinking about it transported me back to the kitchen, T-shirt damp and his fingers combing through my hair. My lips tingled at the memory of the first brush of our lips—his lips really made marshmallows feel like rocks.

Did he regret it? That would explain why things had turned weird and why he was avoiding me. Our texts were as bland as oatmeal, and I hadn't caught a glimpse of him in school.

"The SOS is for emergencies," Peep chastised. "Like, someone's house burning or something."

"Oh, and I broke up with Malia."

"What!" Peep and I said at the same time.

He rolled his eyes. "You called it; it didn't go anywhere."

Peep rubbed the back of his head, and I looked away.

Was it mean to call out the obvious?

Peep cleared his throat. "Sorry."

"Yeah, sorry," I echoed. "That it didn't work out."

"It's—" Mo's face drooped. "Me too."

"What happened?" I asked.

He sat on the bed. "The vibe was all wrong. It was super awkward, like, all the time. I thought it was normal, first date things, and it would go away. It didn't."

"But you liked Malia for two years." Peep held up two fingers. "You did all those things for her! You bought her stuff! We had to stand in line to get a signature from that author with the Merlin beard... I don't understand."

"I know! Turns out we were boring as a couple. There was no chemistry, so we broke up."

"For real this time or...?" Peep asked skeptically.

"Yes, for real."

I rubbed his back. "Sorry it was a waste."

"Not a waste. It was better than nothing. I'm glad I know her." He grabbed two books and stood. "Anyway, you guys can help me get rid of these."

I dropped my jaw. "Wait—what? That's it?"

"I don't want a pity party."

"It's not a pity party, it's expressing your feelings."

"Thanks, Peep. When did you open your therapy practice?" Peep glowered at Mo until he cracked. "Okay, it sucks, but at this point I'm kind of used to it. I'll watch Titanic later and feel better. Happy?"

Peep wrapped his arms around Mo, who tried to duck but reacted too late. I joined in, throwing myself on them.

"This is the last time I allow this," Mo said before shoving us away. "Next time, I'll activate instant decapitation."

"So you're not doing this because you have a broken heart?" Peep asked.

"I don't have a heart."

"But for real?" I asked.

"No, it makes me feel good, and the books need to go either way."

*

It occurred to me Adam wasn't the only one playing the eluding game when I saw him in the hall as I waited for Peep to put his books in his locker and head to lunch. I squeaked and quickly maneuvered to Peep's left, so I had my back to Adam.

To be clear: I was not going out of my way to avoid him. I might even argue I was doing it because *he* was doing it. I was also scared he was doing it because—what if he didn't like guys? What if he did like guys but didn't like me? What if he thought the kiss was bad, and I had onion breath?

The probability of a second rejection from him made me queasy. Another part of me was sure a rejection would be for the best. What if I screwed up a relationship with him? But what if I didn't?

I'd been running this "what if" song in my mind for too long without coming to a solid conclusion, only a shaky one where I let Adam decide, and I'd go with the flow. The problem was, I dreaded an encounter with him—but again, I was *not* actively ignoring him.

Peep glanced over my shoulder and back to me. "What did you do now?"

"Nothing." Adam kissed *me*; I only returned it.

"Really?"

"Okay, something happened…"

"And?"

"I can't tell you."

"Hmm," Peep said. "He started seeing someone else, and you got consumed by mad jealousy and erased him from your life?"

"Not funny." I glared at him. I didn't like how that sounded like the origin story of a TV drama's antagonist.

"True. It was—"

"Pathetic?"

"Mostly, yeah, but I was looking for gentler wording." His eyebrows shot up. "Oh, he's headed this way."

I stiffened. "Tell me you're joking."

"Nope."

"Do I have time to run?" I asked in a panic, seriously considering it.

"Nope— Hey Adam!" he said.

"Hey."

His voice made my skin tingle.

Why did he have to smell good too? I inclined my head a little to look at him. Our eyes met. My stomach fluttered.

"Can we talk?"

Peep grinned. "See you later."

Please don't leave. "Sure," I said hoarsely.

We found a room that was emptying for lunch and ducked inside. I stood opposite him, eyes not meeting and hand twitching at my side. Adam had a blank expression that brought Frida to mind—was she giving out lessons?

"So," I started at the same time as he said, "Listen."

We fell silent.

He cleared his throat. "You didn't make it on Sunday."

"Yeah, I had...stuff I was doing."

"It's not because...we kissed, is it?"

I shook my head. "No, no."

Adam pinched his lips together.

"It's not." I held on to the straps of my bag. "I went to see my ex."

"Oh, you still talk to your ex?"

"Umm, no. There's...stuff I had to tell him."

"To get back together?" Adam asked.

"No, no, no." I pinched the bridge of my nose. "It's... I went to apologize for the way I ended things." I huffed. "I kind of, umm, ghosted him when—when he... confessed his, uh, feelings."

"Oh?"

Adam worried his lip, drawing my attention to his mouth. His lips had been so soft pressed against mine. His body and mine nearly molded together. His hands in my hair. A shiver ran through me.

He released the lip when he noticed me staring and then passed his tongue over it. The space between us crackled with heat.

Adam finally said, "We kissed," pulling me out of my daze.

"Mhmm."

"I liked it."

"Yeah, me too." Could we please do it again?

Adam rubbed the back of his neck. "I'm...I'm not sure I'm ready to, uh, be with someone right now."

"Yeah, okay." I bobbled my head and tried to ignore my heart sinking to the floor.

It kind of made sense: he'd gotten off a long-term relationship, and I was freshly single. Even with that rationality, I had to press a hand to my middle to stifle the disappointment.

"It's the whole Sarah thing, and I don't think I'm there yet. It's not because you're a guy..."

"Yeah, I get it." I tried for a smile, but for some reason, it resulted in my eyes prickling with unshed tears.

Who's to know if we would work anyway? Adam was too self-assured, arrogant; he grinned too much, and when he did, the corner of his mouth dimpled and crinkled in an adorable way...

"It's for the best...I guess. You don't like tea. That's a red flag."

Adam cracked a smile. "Tea is honestly flavored water."

My jaw dropped open. "Okay, don't make me break up the friendship."

"Okay, yeah, too far. And you don't get video games."

"Don't at all. So, uh, we would be doomed from the start." We were lying.

"Completely."

I ran a hand through my hair. What now? Instead of answers, I found myself entranced by his inky eyes. They were deep black pools framed by thick dark eyebrows and luscious lashes. Then those lips—the lower one was pink, the top one brown. The chance to nibble on them excited me.

Adam turned in the other direction.

Get it together.

I'd have to add "find a way to tamp down this attraction" to my to-do list.

"So, umm, you should still be coming over, if you want to, but if you don't want to, either, that's okay."

I grinned. "Okay."

Chapter Twenty-One

Not gonna be awkward, I assured myself.

Adam had invited me over to watch a sci-fi movie with the twins—he made sure to emphasize that in his texts, probably to make clear this was a platonic date, and we wouldn't be alone together in the same room. I agreed, eager to find an excuse to leave the house. The weirdness at home had hit a new high when I saw Paul kiss the back of Granma's hand.

One of the twins opened the door and threw her arms around me. Maya? Had to be, she was the overly enthusiastic one. Em poked her head out from the living room and gave me a small wave, then Adam appeared a moment later.

"Hey." The greeting escaped in a breathy whisper caused by the exertion of cycling for twenty minutes from my place to his, not because my heart was stuttering, but because being here was likely a bad idea. I should have given it a month to come to terms with Adam's, uh, very logical explanation on why we shouldn't date because seeing him in a muscle tee had me thinking we were being too rational.

"Hi." Adam bounced his eyes from my head to my toes. I'd worn extra-tight jeans that hadn't made cycling easy but made it worth it seeing Adam flounder. "Glad you came."

"You said sci-fi." I hated sci-fi. "And here I am."

"That's...cool."

A pause.

"Right, movie...this way—oh, popcorn and snacks first." He headed for the kitchen.

Maya grabbed my wrist and made me follow her to the kitchen. "Which one do you prefer for the snack, Skittles or popcorn?" she asked.

"And you have to answer carefully," Em called out.

I glanced at Adam. He shrugged.

"Popcorn?" I said. "Because it's a classic?"

"What did he say?" Em asked.

"Popcorn!" Maya yelled back as she opened a bag of Skittles.

"Did I pass?"

"Yes. Means we don't have share." She grinned, showing bits of candy stuck in her teeth.

As we headed out of the kitchen, Adam's bare arm brushed my quarter-sleeved one and caused an electric current to zap both of us. We jumped apart like startled cats.

"Sorry..." I said.

"It's fine. Science, right? Static force or something? Ha ha."

I rubbed the spot. "Ha ha. Yeah, static force." Whatever that was made my blood sing.

"Right. Ha!"

Our eyes met, and we both turned away. I caught sight of a large family portrait taken when Adam didn't have his lower teeth.

"Umm, why are you guys being weird?" Maya asked.

"They like each other but don't know what to do with it," Em said in a stage whisper.

I'll burst into flame. Help me! I'll burst into flames.

"Not true," I said.

"We're friends," Adam said.

"Yeah, really good friends. Platonic friends. The best of friends."

Oh God. If I'd known this would be this awkward, I'd have volunteered to clip Granma's toenails.

Maya grinned. "You know, I just remembered we have to do something."

"Oh?" Em asked.

"Mhmm." Maya held Em's gaze.

"You're right!"

They stood in unison, bag of Skittles in hand.

"Umm, where are you going?" Adam sat up quickly, nearly knocking the bowl of popcorn over.

"To do...something we forgot to do," Em said.

Adam's eyebrows shot up. "What? You guys said you were free and *bored*, like, an hour ago. So I invited Rasheed over."

"That's what the meaning of forget is," Em said.

"So we're going to do that thing which we forgot to do."

"What thing exactly?" I asked. "Can I help?" The awkward had to be avoided at all costs.

"It's girl things."

"You guys can still watch the movie though."

They skipped out the room, giggling like Disney villains. The little snakes. They did this on purpose.

"Still want to watch?"

"I guess."

The space between us on the couch seemed as wide as an ocean and yet so suffocating. I pulled on my shirt, which was in the process of gluing to my skin. We were still in the credit scenes. This was going to be so long.

Natalie came into the room several minutes later, and we visibly sighed in relief. Adam thought fast and invited her to join us, which she did. She settled on the couch with us and filled the awkward silence with commentaries that would make dad jokes look like peak comedy. Adam kept asking her to stop, but that only fueled her more. I didn't mind one bit; she managed to make the unease dissipate and set us in easy moods.

Mr. Herman came into the living room in search of Natalie. His eyes zeroed in on Adam. "I hope you're seated there comfortably because you're done with your homework."

"Yes, Dad. I finished it."

"We're relaxing a little. Come join us," Natalie said. Mr. Herman looked from the TV to us.

"I still have work to do." Natalie sighed. "Can I talk to you?"

"We'll leave." Adam stood, and I followed him out of the living room toward his room. "Do you want to see the progress in our game?"

"Yeah," I said enthusiastically. It was what good friends did.

In his room, I collapsed on the second desk chair and scooted closer to Adam, right next to the monitor. Adam booted up the computer, and I took the opportunity to connect to the speaker. I put on my chill playlist, the one I'd clearly sifted through to make sure embarrassing names didn't pop up.

Adam loaded the game. It was a variation of Chrome's dinosaur game—which I'd gone a very long time believing was a chicken—except with a human trying to avoid the dinosaur. He explained how everything worked; it, literally, required only two keys, but even that, I couldn't manage. Like, a noodle could do better. Adam smothered his laugh and even offered to help. He'd press one key, and I'd press the other. Somehow, I became worse. Every time our fingers brushed, my mind went fuzzy. God. It was getting hot.

Beside me, Adam started quaking with laughter. "You're really bad at this."

"I mean, I did say I was."

"No, like, really bad. Maya and Em have better scores." He laughed some more, head thrown back, hand on his chest. His laugh was almost as infectious as Maya's, except he was laughing at me.

"I'll put a sock in your mouth if you don't shut it."

"Okay. Okay."

I got up and settled on one of the beds. Some space was needed if my brain had to continue functioning.

Adam swiveled toward me and tapped my foot with his. "Come back; I'll try to teach you."

"I'm hopeless."

A dimple appeared at the corner of his mouth. "Yeah, but I can teach you to not be as bad."

"How generous."

"I try."

"Okay, but no laughing."

"Promise."

"You realize our promises are shit?"

Adam quirked his lips. "You mean *your* promises. I won't laugh as much."

I got back on the chair, and he dragged it closer, so my knee bumped his thigh.

"Okay, we'll go slowly."

Slow was painful. It meant Adam's hand was on mine a lot, our arms touching. And once, he squeezed my knee to compliment me, and I squirmed. He did it as a reward every time I did well, then, after the fourth time, he let it rest there.

"See, now you don't look like my great-aunt Belle."

I turned to him. "You're comparing me to a what? An eighty-year-old with arthritis?"

Adam grinned. "She's eighty-four now."

"Like that makes it better."

"I just said you don't look like her."

Oh God. We were too close. His arm on my thigh burned a hole through my jeans.

"I got to get home."

His expression fell. "Okay."

I got up, and Adam stood to follow. Before I reached for the door, I remembered something. "I brought you a present."

Adam cocked his eyebrows.

I dug into my pocket and produced a bracelet of strung beads, spelling out "I love tea." I'd paid Tani to make it for me.

Adam took it and inspected it. He read the words and laughed. "Seriously?"

"Consider wearing it as an apology. Now, your hand."

"My hand?"

"So I can put it on you."

He handed the bracelet back, and I put it on excruciatingly slowly. Adam's breath hitched, and from this angle, the bulge in his sweats was hard to ignore. I blinked, focused on the task.

I met his eyes. "There."

"I want to kiss you," Adam said quietly.

My eyes widened.

"Is that okay?"

I nodded. Yes. Yes, please. He took tentative steps toward me, and I held my breath, my eyes entranced with his.

He put his hands on my hips and pressed close. I shivered.

"You good?"

"Yes, now kiss me."

His lips were soft. He paused, shifted his head, and I opened my mouth and sucked in his lower lip.

"Did I mention you have amazing lips?"

"No, but do it more often."

I walked back into the room. Settled on the bed and pulled a startled Adam onto my lap. "This okay?"

"I like it." His lips trailed my neck, nibbling and sucking. I threw my head back to give him more space. I fisted the sheets.

"Can I touch your ass?"

Adam's chuckle burrowed under my skin, and I curled my toes in pleasure. "Yes."

OhGodThankYou. Thank you.

His ass was softer than I expected; I dug my nails right in. He hummed in pleasure as his mouth found mine again.

"I've got a confession to make," I said.

Adam pulled back. "What?"

"I liked you back then."

"Hmm?"

"Before you dated Sarah, I had a crush on you too."

"You're joking."

"I'm not."

Adam frowned. "But..." He studied my face. "You never said anything."

"You didn't either."

He huffed. "Wow, I don't believe it."

"Believe it."

"Worst timing ever, four years too late."

"I know." I kissed his mouth. Planted another on his cheek, then his chin until he was pliant enough for us to really get into it. "But let's get back to this."

Chapter Twenty-Two

I nearly dropped my cup of tea when I saw Adam's texts. The tea was to give me energy for the calculus homework I was about to start on.

> ADAM: *my whole family is at home for like the first time in forever*

> ADAM: *should I tell them all at once? And be done with it today? I'm tempted.*

> ADAM: *fuck it I'll do it*

> ADAM: *I'll tell them I'm bi*

> ADAM: *holy shit!!!*

> ADAM: *why does it feel like someone turned on a vacuum cleaner in my gut?*

> ADAM: *I'm gonna vomit. Is that normal?*

Desperation flared in my chest. I wanted to be there for him.

I chewed on my lip. I had one more hour to go before I could take a break. I tapped on the phone's screen.

ME: *It's normal*

ME: *Do you want me to come over*

ADAM: *we're clearing the guest room...the garage is next. If you want to carry some heavy stuff with a bunch of rowdy guys, sure??*

ME: *I meant for the other thing*

ADAM: *yeah, come hold my hand ☺ under the table though*

My own coming out had been dramatic. Granma had wailed and asked God why before she finally calmed down enough to form coherent words. But then she'd patted my hand and hugged me tight and said, "Okay, it's okay." Which had cracked me open and sent tears spilling down my face.

I'd been fourteen, right after Adam and Sarah had made it official, and I'd wanted to tell someone I was gay.

Telling Peep had been more frightening; I'd lost one friend and was afraid to lose another. He'd been confused at my lack of attraction for boobs, which he viewed as one of the best things to ever exist, but he'd accepted it with a shrug and given me an awkward side hug. I never bothered coming out to Frida, sure she didn't care. If she knew, she knew.

The Herman brothers were in the driveway loading a pickup truck with boxes. The boys were something out of a wet dream—big, muscular, glowing brown skin— Wally with large toned arms, Leo with his cute round glasses, Izzy with short locks and a vine tattoo on his neck. And Adam was Adam, those lips, that body, which I'd explored more of this week.

Adam gave me a side hug, his lips brushing my neck. Wally crushed me in a hug and marveled at how I'd grown. Leo patted my shoulder and mentioned it had been a while. Izzy laughed at Adam for being inches shorter than me, which earned him a jab from Adam, and they got into a wrestling match with Adam in a headlock, the sleeveless tee he wore riding high to show his stomach.

Leo poked Adam's stomach. "You've been getting freaky, baby bro?"

On his stomach was a hickey from when I'd nibbled too hard, which we'd both enjoyed. There was a sense of pride at seeing it there.

"What?" Adam rasped as he tried to get free. "Let me go, asshole."

Wally laughed. "Looks like he has."

Adam managed to get free, and Wally put us to work. We put in the last of it, and drove it to a Salvation Army, and then unpacked it all. I couldn't believe they'd been doing this all day; my arms were aching already, and I wanted to lie down and not wake up until tomorrow.

*

"Thanks for coming," Adam said when we got back to his room. I fell on the bed, and he fell right beside me.

I clamped my hand onto his and squeezed. "You know I'd be here otherwise. Are you still going to come out?"

Adam nodded. "Yeah."

"Okay, now this is going to sound very self-centered but please don't waste time calling me out on it."

"I won't."

"Are you doing this because of umm...us? If you are, you don't have to."

"I'm not." He brought our joined hands up and kissed my knuckles. "It's for me."

"Did you talk to Wally?"

"We were supposed to meet next week, so, no." Adam sighed. "Though I'm pretty sure he'd encourage me to come out. I think partially to piss off Dad."

I rubbed my thumb over his hand. "If it's not safe for you, don't come out."

"Mom's cool, you know? I'm not worried about my brothers because I know Wally would kick their asses—and then patch them up." He snorted. "The twins know."

I pulled him into a tight hug that could help reassure him.

*

We succeeded in getting Wally alone by convincing him to come up to Adam's room for a little chat. Of all the

Herman siblings, Wally looked like Mr. Herman the most. They both had a square jaw, the lighter shade of skin color, hazel eyes, and a piercing gaze that made you want to check yourself. I sat on one of the desk chairs, and Adam was on his bed. It was an attempt at giving him space even though I wanted nothing more than to hold him tight.

Wally's eyebrows knitted together, and he fixed that gaze on Adam. "Adi, you alright?"

Adam straightened. "I'm fine."

"You sure?" Wally reached out his hand to take Adam's temperature, but Adam swatted him away.

"Yes. Please sit."

"You look a little blue."

Adam exhaled, glanced my way with the question in his eye, and back to Wally. "I have to tell you something. Please sit."

Wally's shoulders tensed. "Okay." The bed creaked slightly as his weight settled on it.

"I'm bisexual," Adam said, and Wally did the Herman eyebrow arch. "And I want to come out today."

The tension in Wally's shoulders eased, and then his shoulders straightened. "You're attracted to guys?"

"Mhmm, and girls."

Wally started to crack his knuckles. "Are you sure you want to come out? If you're being pressured to come out—" Here, he turned and gave me a pointed look with the same intensity I'd seen on Mr. Herman. "—don't do it."

Adam rolled his eyes. "Yes, I'm ready, and no, no one is pressuring me, so—"

"I have to warn you, coming out isn't something you do today and then shelve it."

Adam blew out air and turned to me. I gave him an encouraging nod.

"So," Wally went on. "With that in mind, I want to warn you Dad might be a dick—"

"I know," Adam mumbled. He seemed smaller than usual.

Wally clapped his shoulder. "It might take time for him to process. But, be sure I'll have your back, baby bro."

"Thanks, Wally," Adam said quietly.

"So when do you want to do it?" Wally asked.

Adam was silent for a while. "Umm, now."

"That's brave of you," Wally said, and that earned a mega eye roll from Adam. Wally grabbed a pillow and aimed it. "It is, you punk. Now do you have a game plan?"

"Yeah, to just say it."

Wally sighed. "Whenever you're ready—today or ten years from now."

Adam smiled. "Okay."

"Now come on; let's go down before mom realizes we're missing and starts yelling." Wally stood, and we followed him out the room.

Natalie handed Adam and me potatoes to peel as soon as we stepped in the kitchen. Adam was too jittery. His hold on the potatoes kept slipping as we worked. I poked his side in an effort to get him out his head. He squirmed, his body curving into a *C*. I laughed.

Adam weighed the potato with a smirk. "You wouldn't."

"I might," I said.

"Adam you either peel that potato or chop the onions," Natalie ordered.

Next time, he mouthed, going back to peeling the potato.

At the table, Em handed me a plate. "Here, we made sure you got the most."

I took the plate. It had four strips of bacon. "Oh my God, guys. This is so sweet."

"You're welcome," Maya singsonged.

"Uh, guys." Adam cleared his throat. Everyone seated at the table turned their attention to him. "I want to tell you something."

Mrs. Herman put her fork down and straightened her posture.

I tightened my grip on the fork and waited for Adam's next words.

"Okay...here goes." Adam exhaled. "A little disclaimer first. I don't want to hide it any longer. I think if I do, I'm not being honest with you guys, yet you're always insisting we be honest with each other. It's not a big deal—Dad there's no need to overreact."

Mr. Herman shifted on his seat. "I do not overreact."

"You actually do, Dad," Leo said tearing into a rib.

"All the time," Izzy intoned. He tipped his chin at Adam. "So what is it?"

"Alright. Imbithereisaiditnowyouknow."

The table fell silent. My eyes bounced around to Mr. Herman. He seemed—confused.

"What?"

"I heard—he's ugly, and he knows we know," Izzy said.

"Oh, I know! You're not going to college?" Maya said.

"No. I mean—maybe. I haven't—" Adam started.

"What?" Mr. Herman barked.

Adam fidgeted with the cutlery.

God. This was going off tangent. I should speak up— and say what? My words would come out like vomit.

"Is that what you wanted to tell us?" Natalie asked in a gentler tone. They really had good cop, bad cop down to a *T*. "You have something else you want to do?"

Mr. Herman spun in his seat to face Natalie. "Surely, you can't be encouraging him. Natalie, he has been babied enough. Now, he's out here thinking he can skip college. Not in this house."

"Dad, you're overreacting," Leo said. He'd put the bone aside, but his lips had a distracting shine to them that reflected the warm light. It was distracting.

"Overreacting?" Mr. H. fixed Leo with a withering glare. Leo lifted his arms in surrender.

"Reacting too much?" Izzy suggested.

"I'm bisexual!" Adam said in his outside voice.

The room filled with a saturated silence. I held my breath as Mr. Herman's eyebrows shot up to his hairline.

"I knew it!" squealed Em in utter delight.

"Holy shit, baby bro!" Leo said. "For real?"

"Yeah," Adam said.

Mr. Herman cocked his head. "I'm sorry," he said in a low growl. He pushed his plate aside. "I didn't catch that."

Blood rushed in my ears. I sent a silent prayer to the universe, *please don't let this turn into a disaster*.

"Michael—" Natalie started.

"Give me a minute, Nat," he said sharply before he turned his gaze back to Adam. "You like men."

"And women."

Mr. Herman pinched the bridge of his nose. Natalie reached out her hand, placed it on top of his, and squeezed. He clenched his fist. "And you're not doing this to push my buttons?"

Natalie snatched her hand away. "Michael, how can you ask that?"

"Dad, trust me when I say this has nothing to do with you," Wally said.

Mr. Herman went on as if Wally hadn't spoken. "He's been snobbish and standoffish, doing things to rile me up. You think I haven't noticed? You're acting out." He stabbed the air with his index finger.

Adam fisted his hands. "No, Dad. I actually like dick."

The twins gasped. Mr. Herman ground his jaw and squared his shoulders. I became as rigid as ice, nauseous and scared. I wanted to leave.

Natalie reacted first. "Adam, this is the last time you get to speak in a vulgar manner to either of us." The softness in her eyes was gone. "Are we clear?"

"I'm sorry," Adam mumbled.

Mr. Herman opened his mouth. Natalie cut him off. "Don't, Michael. You started this." Mr. Herman's eyebrows shot up. Natalie arched hers and narrowed her eyes. "You invalidated him. Coming out is not easy, and you dismissed him and his sexuality."

After a moment of baited breaths, Mr. Herman said, "You're truly..."

"Bisexual? Yes."

He flattened his palms on the table. "And you're not going to college?"

"I didn't say that."

Mr. Herman reached for the wine, thought better of it and put it down. "Natalie, can we talk?" The chair scraped the floor as he got up. "Now, please."

"Fine."

He walked out the dining room. Natalie stood. She went to Adam, who sat one seat down across from her, and planted a kiss on his forehead. "I love you, okay, no matter what. You know that?" He nodded. She cupped his chin and tilted it upward. "Your dad loves you too." Adam pinched his lips together. "The tough exterior makes it hard to see it. Okay?"

Acid trickled into my heart. I palmed my chest to stop the ache and squeezed my eyes to hide the sting of the tears.

"Yeah," Adam whispered.

She left. I shoved the whatever that was aside and met Adam's eyes. I projected thoughts of calm and ease. Em, who sat on his right, threw herself around him for a hug; Maya did the same. We joined in on the group hug.

"How are you keeping up?" Wally asked.

"What mom said; he'll come around," Leo assured him.

"I need a moment."

We watched him walk away. The front door opened and closed. I counted to fifty before I got up and went after him.

He was pacing.

"Hey, how are you doing?"

"An absolute-fucking mess." He tugged on his hair. "I need to get out of here."

"To where?"

"I don't know."

"Let's start walking then."

Chapter Twenty-Three

"That was a complete disaster." I nudged Adam with my shoulder as we continued down the sidewalk. Our aimless walk had led us deeper into the neighborhood, each house farther than the last, but it was quiet with only the occasional bark of a dog.

Adam kicked an invisible rock. "It was."

"Not like totally, but it was not so bad."

"It was the worst." He narrowed his eyes.

"Not like your dad wasn't—"

"An ass?"

"Umm, yeah. Your mom was cool though."

"I know. I wish Dad was more like her. He makes me doubt myself, you know?"

"Trust me, I know."

"Right." He peeped at me from under his lashes. "Your— Frida?"

A lump formed in my throat. "Aha."

"How's that going?"

"Nowhere." As usual. "But maybe to the airport when she leaves." She would. It was only a matter of time. "I might even drive her to the airport."

The anger was hot on my tongue.

"You don't drive."

"I might learn that day."

"Why is that anyway?"

"I want to reduce my carbon footprint in the world, and biking is good for your heart."

"Ha!" he said. "But really though?"

I shrugged. "That's the bonus." I cleared my throat. "I'm bad at it."

"We all start off bad."

"No, like, I'm bad. I failed the test," I mumbled.

Adam stopped in the middle of the sidewalk and cried out, "You failed a test?"

"Announce it to everyone, don't you?" I tugged him forward. "Not one of my proudest days, but to be fair, the supervisor was reeking of tobacco, and it was pretty distracting."

He fluttered his eyelashes.

"It's not an excuse. I hate the smell of tobacco. It distracted me enough that I hit a signpost."

His jaw dropped. "You did not."

"Did too."

"You weren't hurt or anything, right?"

"No, I wasn't."

"Good."

Adam angled his head, aiming a kiss on my cheek. I tilted my head a bit, and his lips brushed my mouth instead. His lips stretched into a smile that made my stomach do a backflip before he deepened the kiss. I gasped. The street was dark and empty, but a nosy housewife could poke her head out the window and see us.

When we let go, we were breathless. "I think I'm ready to head back."

No. Not yet. "Is it okay if we stay a little longer?"

"Sure, let's take the scenic route."

We held hands and continued down the street, blanketed in comfortable silence.

The day's events played in my mind; each week *was* getting longer. But this: the fresh air, the quiet, and Adam's hand clasped in mine was nice. Maybe there was something to walks; I needed more of them in my life.

My contentment got doused a few minutes later when Natalie came to mind. Her eyes had shone down on Adam with love. Strong, steady love. She wasn't unsure; she loved Adam. She loved all six of them and didn't grow tired of doing it.

What was that like?

I wouldn't know. She didn't care for me, and she probably never had.

Maybe she had. Maybe even now, she did. I didn't know. I couldn't know for sure because I didn't know Frida well.

But did she care for me—if I had to think about and try to convince myself?

She was a bad mother; there was not much else to it.

I heaved a sigh.

"What?"

I palmed my face with my free hand. "I'm brooding. Mood feels right."

"Why?"

"Thinking about Frida. I am not angry enough at her slacking on her...her mom duties."

"Rasheed—"

"But then what? I don't want to think about someone who neglected me every minute."

"You're right. She'd only eat up your energy."

"I want to know *why*. Why Granma looked after me and did everything for me when I had a mother right there doing nothing."

My breath caught. I stopped and forced a large inhale and slowly exhaled. "When—when my grandfather abused Granma... I'd broken a cup, and he was in a mood.

He wanted to teach me a lesson, but Granma had said no… I keep thinking maybe if I had a mom, nothing like that could have happened.”

Adam swung his arms around me and buried his head in my neck. I snuggled into him. “I'm sorry you had to go through that. But it's not your fault. I don't think anything you could have done could have made Frida stay.”

He kissed my cheek.

“Our parents come with all kinds of garbage; that's what Mom told me. Dad's hard on us because he grew up poor. His dad came back paralyzed by PTSD from the Vietnam War. He'd sit all day doing nothing. Mom says that's why he likes us being active and why he's a hard-ass. It's not entirely my fault even though I antagonize him sometimes. It's a back-and-forth thing—a tennis match.”

“I think your mom is, like, the best thing ever,” I mumbled into his neck.

“We can share her.”

“I'd like that.” I pressed into him. “Let's stay like this forever.”

“I'm with you, but can we sit down? I think we've been walking for at least a week, and I am tired.”

“I don't think it's even been an hour. Don't you exercise?”

“I lift weights. Even I'm not crazy enough to do cardio.”

An oak tree stood a few feet away and a little off the road. We decided to break there. I sat against the tree, and Adam rested against my chest. I had one arm under him and the other tucked beneath his shirt, touching solid muscle. I poked his sides.

"God, don't," he squealed.

"Only because you squealed."

"Fuck you."

I titled my head to lean on the oak. The stretch of empty grassland before us and the wide, dark sky hanging over us made for a beautiful portrait. "I've always wanted a date under the stars."

"Really?"

"Kind of. I mean it sounds poetic."

"Hmm."

I cupped his cheek. "What?"

"We've never been on an official date."

I laughed. "How'd we miss that?"

"I'd christen this as a date, but the day was too shitty."

"This part is not bad at all."

He smiled. "True."

Chapter Twenty-Four

By the time we got back, four hours had passed, and the parents were *not* happy. We would have been aware of the time if we'd remembered to take our phones. Adam had left his charging, and mine was in my hoodie left on his bed.

The word "disappointment" was hauled out by Natalie, a lot. I won't lie; it hurt. Wally had to take me home because Natalie was too fraught to drive. And home would be worse. I'd stayed out most of the night. Hadn't answered calls and texts. To Granma, that was sufficient grounds for murder.

She met me at the porch, hands on her hips, heaving as if she'd run a marathon. "Did we not talk about this? Huh?"

"I'm so sorry, but I forgot my phone."

"*Anajaribu kuniua,*" she told Paul. "He's trying to kill me. He's giving me high blood pressure."

Before, I would have rolled my eyes, but it wasn't her exaggerating anymore. She'd had a stroke. The guilt persisted.

"Come, sit down." Paul took her elbow and maneuvered her to the closest seat.

"I'm sorry—"

She held up her hand. "We'll discuss this tomorrow."

I sighed and started for my room. "Okay."

Frida stood in my way, dressed in purple silky pajamas. I did a double take; up to this point, I was convinced she slept in her beloved khakis.

Our eyes met. Resentment hardened my heart.

"Are you hungry?"

"No." I said sharply.

She winced.

I sidestepped her and stomped to my room.

*

Granma being at church did not equal a calm state of being.

I prepared for the worst. A very long tirade where she'd switch between English and Swahili as she shamed me for my behavior. Her guilt-tripping me, which always worked for, like, two weeks—I'd do all my chores on time, rinse a cup and put it away when done with it, and not leave my shoes lying around.

The reality was different. Granma walked in, vibrating with exhaustion. Her eyes were heavy-lidded, there were more lines and wrinkles on her face than before, and her shoulders were hunched. She'd had a ministroke and surgery, yet here I was, stressing her. How could I have forgotten?

"I'm sorry," I blurted out, my voice cracking.

She took a seat next to me on the bed. "I heard what happened with Adam. I understand he needed a friend. But that didn't mean you had to disobey my rules."

"I know. I'm sorry. We left our phones in the house, and we lost track of time."

"And do I want to know what you were doing, or will it make me want to grab my slippers?"

I concentrated on my blue rug, poking at it with my big toe. It hadn't been that bad, but I wasn't keen on enlightening her, either, because she'd ruin it. I would frame the memory if it were possible.

"Eedy, I hope I don't have to remind you how your education comes first."

"I know." I knew too well.

"Here, you have a chance, an equal and fair chance to make it. Please don't get sidetracked."

"I know. I'm sorry. It won't happen again."

"I'm not only talking about yesterday. I'm talking about how distant you have been. When the school year started, you made a plan, remember? To put all your attention on school, but I've not seen the same commitment you had started out with."

"It's been a rough couple of weeks."

"You might have a point. Is this about Paul?"

I shook my head.

"I meant it—if you were uncomfortable, I would end it. My father remarried, and I didn't have a say in it at all, and it turned into a complete disaster. My stepmother was a snake."

I'd met her. She had a pointy nose and liked to think she had authority over everyone.

"No, it's not about Paul," I said. We didn't speak about it aloud, so the words took longer to form in my mouth, but I couldn't push it away any longer. "It's Frida."

"Oh," she exhaled. I'd touched on a taboo topic.

"We never talk about it."

"I know."

"And now she's staying? I don't know what to make of it."

Granma wrung her hands. "Yes, we have never talked about it. I thought...you didn't know."

"I knew. A year after we moved here, I remember you asking her to stay, so we could be a family, so she could raise me. But she left the next day, and we didn't see her for months."

"I want you to know it's not you. Frida has her own demons she has to fight, but she refuses to." She clicked her tongue in disgust.

"I keep hearing that. Doesn't mean she had to put that on my shoulders too. I don't deserve it."

"No, you don't." She paused. "I'm sorry about Frida. I tried to make her stay and be a mother."

If she had asked more than once, then Frida had refused more than once. The world pressed down on me. But why?

"Having someone who is supposed to care for you neglect that duty—it's the worst kind of heartbreak. It tears you apart, and it sets someone on a rocky path." She reached out for my hand and squeezed it. "It's hard to accept this, but it's not you; try to remember that. Not you, it's them.

"I remember I tried in every way to please my stepmother. I had it set in my mind if I woke up earlier, if I cleaned the house, took care of her children, basically, if I bent over backward for her that maybe she'd like me a little more. She never did, never." She exhaled. "I mentioned it to my father, and he didn't listen to what I had to say, chalked it up to me being an adolescent or something. It destroyed my self-worth, and that's why I stayed with your Babu long as I did, because I thought I didn't deserve any love. I was wrong."

My heart squeezed. "I'm sorry."

"It's in the past now—*maji yakimwagika hayazoleki*. It's water under the bridge. I don't want you feeling bad because another person doesn't know any decency. I never understood. I didn't influence their behavior; they were always frigid like that. So, I went on with life, believing I deserved the pain because I wasn't good enough."

Tears pricked the corner of my eyes, and I shuddered at the weight of her words.

"I don't want you to go through life thinking like that. I really don't. You are enough. You are the right amount of yourself. You're great just the way you are, okay? Don't ever think different."

Tears rolled down my cheeks.

Granma reached out her large hand, wrapped it around my shoulder, and pulled me to her. I buried myself in her chest and started to sob. "*Ujue nakupenda*," she said quietly, patting my back. "Know that I love you."

I inhaled sharply before I began to quake with sobs. She'd never said it before; this was a first. I knew I had to say it back as well, but the words were tight around my throat, nearly choking me. I did know she loved me. She had stuck with me through everything without ever tiring. She was always there for me.

I held on tighter, never wanting to let go.

My phone buzzed loudly. I'd set it to max volume to alert me when I received a text. The screen lit up to notify me Adam had sent a text. Granma squeezed my shoulder and pulled away.

"How's he doing?"

"We haven't talked yet." I sniffed and wiped away my tears.

She glanced at the phone on my nightstand. "Are you two...together?"

"Not officially." We hadn't discussed it.

Her eyes widened. "You know my opinion on that?"

"Okay. School first, but I think someone can balance both."

"And with the way you're acting irresponsibly, how will you manage?"

"I'm sorry about that. I'll try to be better."

"I still can't believe you made me worry like that. You, Rasheed. Where did I go wrong?" She pulled my ear and let go.

"Ow. I'm sorry."

"If I see even a single slip up with your grades! If I see you acting irresponsibly, there'll be a time-out with you and Adam. Clear?"

"Clear."

She paused. "Are— You know how to use protection, and to use it all the time?"

The back of my neck prickled. Make this end already. "I do."

"*Kumbe.*" She narrowed her eyes. "Oh."

OhmyGod.

She sighed. "When did you grow up? Go back to being nine when you were following me around everywhere." She pulled me into a hug and then let go. "Don't forget your priorities. Is that fair?"

"Mhmm. Okay."

She stood, and the phone buzzed again. She chose to ignore it and gave me one last glance. I squirmed. "Don't forget—it's not you. You are not the problem, and you won't be."

"I won't."

Chapter Twenty-Five

ADAM: *Hey*

ADAM: *sorry I missed your texts. I've been sleeping. How you been?*

ME: *Had a weird conversation with my Granma*

ADAM: *yeah?*

ME: *we finally talked about Frida*

ADAM: *how'd that go*

ME: *it went well ☺ I'm still alive.*

ADAM: *what did she say about Frida?*

ME: *that I shouldn't take it personally*

ADAM: *she's your mom, hard not to take it personally*

ME: *yes, exactly!! But I don't have an option if I want to look after myself. I can't keep waiting for her, you know?*

ADAM: *I get it*

ME: *But what about you?*

ADAM sent a string of a masked emojis.

ADAM: *I'm calling…*

I didn't have enough time to check myself for, like, boogers and stuff before Adam's call came through. His face filled the screen, and he looked crusty, his skin ashen, lips cracked. But he appeared unbothered, like he couldn't give a shit. Still, seeing him made my skin hum with an undercurrent of awareness.

"Hey," he said and rubbed his chin.

"What happened?"

He picked a lock from his hair and twirled it. "Mom was righteously angry, and I mean angry. I got an earful for that. Dad didn't let the opportunity pass him by; he started up on how irresponsible and lazy I am."

I snorted. "They must have been reading from the same script as Granma."

He sighed and pulled at his face. "I told him I'm not interested in the same things he is—politely of course. Mom made us have a very long exhausting talk about my college plans." He rubbed his eyebrows. "Dad brought out a worksheet and started planning everything again. So then we had to talk about that too." He huffed. "The bottom line—I improve my grades, and in exchange, he stops overworking me. It was exhausting."

"But, like, he is okay with you being bisexual?"

Adam twisted his mouth. "Yeah, he says that but...I don't know if he believes me. I guess he's trying? I'm not sure."

"We need hugs."

"I knew I'd get you hooked on them."

I smiled.

Chapter Twenty-Six

I stumbled out of bed and headed for the bathroom, eyes soggy and wet, yawning and trying to rub the crust from my eyes with my nails.

I kicked the bathroom door open, revealing Paul at the sink, washing his face. I shook my head, wondering if I was still dreaming. One time, I'd been dreaming about snakes, and when I finally woke up, they were on my bedroom floor, and when I blinked, they'd disappeared.

Paul stood there, startled. "Rasheed, morning."

"Umm, morning," I said, rattled by his presence. He wore faded track pants and a large shirt, and the outfit said in bold neon letters that he'd just woken up. My brain tried to process that, but it was not fully operational six minutes after I'd woken up from a restless sleep.

He held the door for me. "It's yours now."

I stood at the entrance, unmoving for a minute, my brain trying to decipher how Paul was in our home this early, wearing what I imagined were his pajamas.

When the implication of his presence at six in the morning was processed, I shuddered and gagged because—gross!

So this was really happening? He and Granma? For a moment there, I'd pushed it to the back of my mind, but this was cold water down my back, and my earlier misgivings floated to the top of my head.

I found Paul in the kitchen, his eyes fixed on the coffee machine.

"Hey kid," he said oh-so casually as his hand went to his mouth to cover a yawn.

"Did you stay over?" I asked, trying to stop a wince at the thought of him and Granma sharing... OhmyGod. Brain, please stop. Too much information and I'd break.

Paul smiled, and his eyes crinkled in amusement. "You don't seem ready for the answer."

I considered it and concluded ignorance was bliss. Hearing it stated so plainly would make my brain try to recreate images, and no, I did not need that floating in my mind. "Okay, don't tell me."

Paul laughed silently. "What will it be for breakfast?" He gestured at the coffee pot and then at the bread. "I'm making French toast, after my first cup."

"I'll eat cereal." I let out a big yawn and rubbed my eyes, gritting my teeth to stop a second one as my eyes watered.

"Late night?"

"Not exactly."

More like early morning. Adam and I had talked until morning, neither of us willing to end the call, until we couldn't keep our eyes open any longer. Even then, we hadn't wanted to part ways. Thinking about it made my heart fuzzy and skin warm.

"I heard you laughing all night." Paul poured himself a steaming cup of coffee and took a tentative sip. Granma was like that with tea; she liked it scalding hot. "Rukia wanted to go tell you to shut up, but I told her not to." Paul added a sly grin, and I found myself choking on air.

"Bluh, TMI!"

Paul blew at his coffee. "Relax, your Granma was reading out loud to me about how her writing is going, and you'd burst into laughter, startling us. But I was half asleep most of the time, and finally, when I slept? Best sleep of my life."

"Wow, like, no offense, Paul, that sounds boring."

Paul clapped me on the shoulder. "That's how I like it. I lived fast and furious back then, and I'm happy; I have no regrets. This 'boring' is all I want now, and a beautiful kind woman to push it along."

"If Granma heard you called her boring, you'd get an earful."

"This is between us, then—What on earth! This coffee tastes like wet sand." Paul put the cup down, lips pressed together.

"That's why I stick to my cereal unless I'm desperate," I said.

"We'll get a new machine."

"I like how you said 'we.'"

Paul turned his head sharply. "Is that okay with you? I know Rukia spoke with you but…"

I shifted my feet from left to right and concentrated on pouring milk into the bowl. "Umm, it's okay. I want Granma to be happy, but I have some concerns…"

Paul stood straighter and turned to me, giving me his full attention. "You can tell me."

I huffed out a breath. "Two concerns actually. The first—I'm gay."

I paused a beat and waited for Paul to soak that in. My heart hammered in my chest, and blood rushed in my ears. I hadn't done this in a while—come out—but the moment of pause still made my skin itch. It could be nothing, but then again, it could be something, and maybe I'd end up looked at in a way that is hateful. But right then, I wanted him to accept me for the sake of Granma, who was now always radiant and glowing with happiness.

"That's not a problem from my end. I accept you for who you are. You're still you to me."

The lump in my throat dissolved, and relief flooded my heart. That was out of the way, at least. "Okay, cool. The second thing—I hope you won't take charge of this home just because you're male."

Paul smiled. "Rukia made that very clear, and also won't be a problem. I have no right, and I actually enjoy being a submissive."

Okay...I hoped my brain would chuck that in the bin before it found its way into my memory folder.

"Anything else?" Paul asked.

"If you treat her like shit, I won't be held liable for my behavior."

"And I'll deserve it," he said.

"You're quite the smooth talker," I observed.

That earned me a laugh. "I won't deny it got me into trouble a few times."

"Yeah, how?"

Paul regaled me with a tale from his youth about how he'd had some brothers who'd threatened his life when he got a little too friendly with their baby sister, and how he'd had to skip over a short hedge fence to get away.

Granma's hips swayed as she entered the kitchen. The Bluetooth speaker in her hand emitted the shrill voices of female Taarab singers. She mumbled along to the song and continued dancing.

Dear God, it was going to be one of those days.

"Okay, that's it for today." I thanked the heavens there was school to get to.

*

Peep and Mo found me making my way to homeroom. Mo punched my flimsy bicep hard enough that I lost footing. I turned to glare. "What the hell?"

"For not calling, disappearing, and making us worry."

I tried to punch him back, but he ducked, and there was no real energy to it.

"I'll get you for that." I rubbed my bicep. "And it was four hours. I forgot my phone." Which was the sad part. The need for us to be official gnawed at me even if my history with relationships was shit, but I wanted to believe I was more aware now and willing to work through it. I was worth affection, dammit, and I could and would give it back.

"Seems like you're ditching us," Mo said.

"I'm not."

"I was worried, so you know—because that was so not like you."

I groaned. "Peep, stop. You sound like my grandmother."

"Wise and potent, listen to her."

I rolled my eyes.

"And then you had the nerve to ttyl us?" Mo shook his head in disgust. "Do you think you could maybe be good again?"

"I do *one thing.*"

"It could be the start to your villainy arc. Don't underestimate 'one thing.'"

My phone buzzed.

ADAM: *want to meet in a janitor's closet?*

I quickly typed a *yes*.

"I gotta go."

"You owe us for ignoring us."

"Sure, meet at lunch."

*

The janitor's closet smelled like bleach and acid. Adam leaned against a shelf stacked with toilet paper, a lazy smile on his face. "Hey."

"Hey."

"You look like shit."

I laughed. "Same."

I closed the space between us and pulled him into a hug. We held on to each other. His jean jacket smelled like lavender and his hair like mint. His lips brushed over the skin on my neck, and I pulled him closer to me. My body was saying yes, please, and more. Adam gazed up at me with heavy-lidded eyes, his lips soft-looking and parted, calling to me.

I lifted my hand, tilted his head sideways, and dipped down for a kiss. His fingers dug into my back and dragged me closer.

"You okay?" I asked.

"Very much." He licked his lips. "You?"

"I wouldn't mind a bed." The back of my neck prickled. "To sleep."

"I wouldn't mind a bed either." Adam peppered my mouth and neck with kisses, and I encouraged him with little noises of pleasure. This went on for a couple more minutes before we were rudely interrupted by the bell.

Chapter Twenty-Seven

I owe my friends.

The words had been in a thought bubble at the bottom of my weekly schedule, written in neat cursive, next to a doodle of me with an exaggerated round face and hearts for eyes. Peep. He couldn't be trusted with a pen in his hand.

He'd also added a new task to my to-do list. Right below "do laundry" was "meet with my friends."

I pulled out my phone and brought up our group chat. I replied, *okay, I get it. We'll meet. Need to catch up first with my schoolwork.*

A knock came on my door. "May I come in?" Frida asked.

My eyes darted around the room. My bed was unmade, covered with homework and clean laundry. "I guess." She took tentative steps into my room. Her presence in what I considered my safe space startled me. I don't think she'd ever been in here before. "Umm, everything okay?"

She hummed in agreement as her eyes wandered the room, over the rumpled bed also scattered with outfits that hadn't made the cut, the cluttered desk, and the shoes sprawled on the floor, which clearly needed vacuuming. Her eyes landed on mine. "Are you free? I want us to...talk."

This was it, then, the day I got my answers. My gut rolled. I wasn't ready. There was a good chance this could go even worse than last time, and I wouldn't be able to handle it. I thought of saying no, I wasn't ready. But I knew if I refused, I'd probably never get a chance like this again, or maybe I'd have to wait another eighteen years.

"I have time," I said.

She settled on the edge of my bed, directly opposite me, with maybe two inches of space between us once I turned to face her, thanks to our long legs. I couldn't hide; there was no room for that. I couldn't fidget either, afraid of betraying my nerves when she sat there looking stoic and sure. I straightened, then paused and looked at Frida. She did look calm, as though it was another casual day.

I didn't like it. I didn't like the mask of indifference. I didn't want to be a brick wall, emotionless. It wasn't me. I wanted to be like Granma, always looking forward.

But she'd inflicted pain when she chose to leave. How could she not have seen how that could affect me?

"I'm..." She exhaled. "I'm..." She had tired eyes. "Sorry." She flattened her hand on her thigh. "For not being there for you."

My eyes fluttered shut. The words sank, unbidden, and dissolved under my skin. They formed a fuzziness in me and dulled the throbbing in my head. I hadn't realized how much I needed to hear those words until they started to peel away my inhibitions.

"So, your father..." She reached into her hoodie's pocket and produced a thick folded paper and handed it to me. I stared at it for a second or two, hesitant and unafraid, before I reached for it.

It was smooth in my hand with splotches of brown fingerprints. Slowly, I unfolded the paper and found myself gazing at an older version of me, except shorter.

I gasped.

The man stood leaning against a tree. He was in blue shorts, a white shirt, and brown Maasai sandals. His gaze was on the camera and a bright white smile lit his features. God, the resemblance was uncanny, the round face, the deep brown shade of his skin, the soft black curls, the round wide eyes that seemed to always be in a constant state of shock, his round stomach... The only thing that was different was the height.

There was a bubble of something loud and hideous inside me waiting to erupt. I couldn't tell whether it was hysterical laughter or tears.

As Granma liked to say, *mtoto wa nyoka ni nyoka.* An apple doesn't fall far from the tree.

"His name was—Juma Mtalaki. We met at a wedding. I stepped on his shiny black shoes. I turned to apologize..." She looked away. "...and something in my mind clicked into place. We spent the entire ceremony getting to know each other." She laughed. "We didn't spend that much time apart after that. I didn't want to. I'd sworn to focus on school and not be bothered by men until after I got a job." She fisted her hands. "Life had other plans. He was kind, quiet, and patient. The nicest man I've ever met. A year and a half after we met, I got pregnant."

My chest tightened.

"I didn't know what to do; I hadn't thought much about having children. I'd always wanted stability first, but Juma was excited." Tears started to stream down her cheeks.

I blinked in surprise; I'd never seen her emotions on display. I shifted in my seat.

"In the seventh month of the pregnancy, he didn't come home, but I was too tired to notice, and then he wasn't there the next day. There'd been an accident; the *matatu* he'd been in had collided with a truck, and he'd died." Her grief made her voice wobble and fade in some places.

My heart hammered away with the loss of something that could have been.

"Next thing I remember is being in hospital and you in my arms." She wiped away her tears—hers flowed in two straight lines. "You were a big baby with wide eyes like his. I remember being desperate, scared, and full of pain. It was too much, a dead partner and a newborn." She sniffled and used her hoodie to wipe more tears. My own body didn't know how to handle her crying, so I started to cry too. "I ran away, I signed up for a master's scholarship, and when I got in, I left without looking back. I thought the space would give me time to come to terms with everything, but..."

"And it was when I'd see you, the grief would come back. When I got you and Mama to come live with me, I thought I could do it, be a mom to you, but I'd been gone for so long, I thought it didn't matter anymore. So I maintained a distance. I was wrong. I was so wrong. I'm sorry, Rasheed."

My mouth dried as I studied the picture. My father. The echo sounded weird in my mind. I'd gone through life used to knowing I didn't have one. I wanted to scream. I could have had a father if life had been different. He would have cared for me, he'd have been there... The thought got swallowed by a harsh wave of self-doubt. Maybe not, maybe he would have rejected me the same way Frida had. And what would he have done if he found out I was gay?

Did it matter now? It didn't. The universe had given me nothing in the parent department.

Not nothing, a voice whispered in my head. I had my grandmother.

"You were wrong," I said quietly, venom lacing the words. I wiped the tears from my eyes and met hers. "You fucked me up."

Her face contorted into pain. She nodded. "I know, and I was too late in realizing what I'd done."

I glared at the floor, trying to get my mouth to work. "The worst part was waiting for you," I said through a thick lump in my throat. "I was always waiting for you, and when you came, you'd give me nothing, and it hurt. But when you left, I would want you back still. Until I stopped caring because I knew you didn't care for me."

She scooted closer as if to reach for me; I angled away. "I do care. Shame and grief kept me away. You didn't do anything wrong; you were only a child."

"I was. A child without parents."

She swallowed. "I'm sorry; I wish I could do it differently."

"I wish you could too," I said flatly.

"I regret it every day."

I hoped it kept her up all night, the way it had when I was younger. "Why didn't I get my father's last name?"

"I thought it would be easier."

She needed to stop thinking, dammit. It wasn't doing her any favors.

I ran a hand over my face. My father. I tried to create space in my mind for his existence, but it didn't fit. He was a stranger. She hadn't even honored his memory.

What had he seen in her?

Frida. Her wet almond-shaped eyes, her eyelashes clumped together. She had a round wide nose, high cheekbones, and clear brown skin. Back then, she used to have her hair in a bob, but the fade made her look fit for a modeling career. Grace Jones please step aside.

She was too closed off. Was that grief? "You need therapy," I said. *I* needed therapy.

She chewed her bottom lip. "I think you're right."

I folded the picture and handed it back to her. She shook her head. "If you want, you can keep it."

Why not. I placed it inside my desk drawer. I'd buy a frame, put it on my bedside table next to the picture of me on my fifth birthday, Granma looming behind me. I turned to her, ready for the conversation to end. I knew now what I'd always wanted to know. "Is that all?"

"Don't—do you have any questions?"

"Not now." I had to process this stuff first, go over the entire conversation and unpack it slowly.

"I'll...I'll be here for you, in whatever way you want."

I narrowed my eyes at her. "Do you mean that?"

"I do. I'm staying."

I squeezed my eyes shut to keep the tears at bay. I'd wanted to hear that since I was little. Too overwhelmed, I only nodded.

She left, shutting the door gently behind her. I stood and stretched, releasing the tension wrapped around my entire body. My mind was in a daze, an emotional hangover, and my body buzzed with nervous energy.

I knew the truth, and yet the world rotated the same. There hadn't been a tilt in the earth's axis, a shift in air density, or a change in gravity. It was the same. But inside me, plates shifted, things clicked into place and others unlocked to allow a breeze, some light.

I needed to burn off the nervous energy.

I walked out, grabbed my bike, sent a text to Granma telling her I needed to clear my head, and set out. It was dark out, the air cool, perfect for cycling.

I picked up the pace, peddling so fast. My shirt became soaked with sweat. Every part of me ached, but I pushed harder. The road flattened, and I let go of the handlebars. Sweat and tears wet my face. I had answers now. It was not me.

Not me. Not me.

Chapter Twenty-Eight

Mo, Peep, and Tani sat in a booth in a corner of Juicy. Peep and Tani took up one side of the booth, Peep resting his head on Tani's shoulder. They were always touching, their bodies drawn to each other. Sometimes, they didn't even notice it. I wanted something like that, and I wanted to hold it dear in my heart, water and let it grow. Mo sat on the opposite side. The faint smile on his lips disappeared.

"You kept us waiting."

I slid in next to Mo and had to exert a little pressure when he refused to budge. "Sorry, I was having a chat with my group members for a history assignment." Which was somewhat true. There had been a two-minute meeting where we exchanged contacts and promised to communicate more. Adam and I had also spent some quality time making out in his car.

"You're lying," Tani accused.

Aurora, our favorite waitress, came over with a big smile and took our order and spent an extra minute aimlessly teasing me for growing my hair out. "Pretty boy, you look cute."

I covered my face with both hands. "I forgot to go to the barber."

"For weeks?" She pinched her lips together. "Who are you trying to impress?"

Nope, I did not think of Adam saying repeatedly how he liked his fingers going through my hair. "No one."

Aurora winked. "Aha, anyway, same old?" she asked turning to the others.

Mo slid closer to me after Aurora left and sniffed me like an eager dog. I inched away, eyes narrowed on him. "Why are you being weird?"

"*You* smell weird."

"Weird?" I asked, nosing at my shirt. Underneath the scent of detergent, there was a hint Adam's new cologne—made sense, with how close we'd been pressed—and, of course, the smell of incense. You'd think since we weren't so close to a body of water, which according to Granma meant a haven for bad spirits, that she'd stop with the incense.

"Nice, actually. Like, not a Granma," Mo said and the others burst into laughter.

"I'll fuck you up, Mo, I swear."

Mo clapped my shoulder. "Okay, sorry..."

I shrugged off his touch and put a few inches between us. "How'd we become friends again?"

Mo was Peep's friend first, and Mo had thought Peep was a pretty girl because of his curly Afro and soprano voice. Peep was pretty, his skin a beautiful shade of deep brown, and he had long eyelashes. Mo had tried to woo Peep, which was the funniest thing at the time, and something he liked to pretend never happened. Once Mo's interest in Peep died, he became a friend. I didn't mind because Mo wasn't an ass about me being gay, and we'd shared a bit of an obsession for Captain America fanfiction.

"Let's not," Peep groaned and palmed his face. "Prepuberty was so fucked up for me."

"But you were so pretty," Mo teased.

"The fairest of them all," I added.

"Like, you were so lovely," Tani said, moving to plant a kiss on Peep's forehead. Peep turned his head and caught it on his lips with a smirk. The tenderness of the act made my heart long for the same. I wished Adam were here, but he and Eric were tinkering with their game, and even if Adam had come, would he have let me touch him like that in public? We weren't boyfriends, and this was what people in relationships did. I wanted it. I was ready for it, for him. I wanted Adam to be too.

"You know what's more interesting?" Peep asked. "The hickey on Rasheed's neck."

The bastard.

I raised my hand to cover the spot.

"Other side," Tani added amused.

I splayed my hand over the left side and felt the tenderness. Another dark, ugly mark from Adam, the fucker. I bit down on my lip to stop the stupid smile from blossoming. At some point, Adam and I would have to get a tetanus shot or something.

"Let me see," Mo insisted as he reached to pull my hand out of the way. I resisted. It was none of his business. "So, what, you'll eat like this?"

I dropped my hand, and Mo, who sat on my right, craned to get a look at my left side. "Fuck, that's ugly. Is he some extra from some vampire show or what?"

"I have concealer if you want," Tani offered, already reaching into her bright pink bag. "Though I'd have to, like, do the rest of you so it can blend in."

"You're totally using that as an excuse to do my makeup."

Tani shrugged. "In my head, I'd contour those cheekbones to make it look like they'd cut through rocks."

"Maybe another time."

Tani pouted. "You always say that."

"So who's the guy? Not Scott, though, right?" Mo asked. "I understand you apologized, but that'd be fucked up."

I froze for a second, panic starting to rumble in my gut. Adam was only out to his family and friends. Oh, and Peep knew, but that had been all Peep. I didn't want to out the guy; that would be assholish. Nevertheless, I hated that was the reason I had to keep it on the down-low…that it was none of their business, sure.

"Says the guy who's on and off with some girl who uses him," Tani said behind a cough, saving me from answering the question. From how fast her gaze left me, I knew she knew.

Of course, Peep would tell Tani. They acted like an old married couple and shared everything between them.

"Shut up, I'm over that. Moving on to greener pastures."

"Mhmm," Tani said.

Aurora brought the sandwiches, and we were silent as we dug into our meals. The conversation moved to Tani's tennis match before Mo came back around to the hickey issue.

"So this vampire, is it serious?" Mo flicked my ear to grab my attention. "Boyfriend serious?"

Heat crawled down the back of my neck. "Umm it's new and shit, so, like, I don't want to talk about it."

Mo blew out his cheeks. "So nothing interesting to talk about, you mean." I punched his arm, and he snickered. "Anyway, how do you know when another guy likes you?"

"Aww, Mo, is this you coming out to us?" Tani asked, eyes wide and arm already outstretched to offer comfort.

Mo snatched his arm away. "Don't 'aww' me, and call it what you want. I'm just asking. I've been talking to a guy on IG, and he asked me about the shirt I had on—it had an anime character—but it started getting personal." Mo stuffed some fries in his mouth and bounced his eyes around the food on the table. "Like, I hear from him more than I do your ugly asses—"

"My ass is very pretty, thank-you very much," Tani cut in.

"—and sure, I never mind having more friends with...refined tastes." Mo grabbed his phone from the table and did a quick job of opening his Instagram.

Tani rolled her eyes until only the whites were visible. "You're so insufferable."

"Shit!" Mo exclaimed and burst into laughter. "I think I know who the vampire is. I'm happy for you, and weirded out a little, but happy for you." He put his arm around my neck and pulled me in for a smothering hug, some of my sandwich fillings starting to fall out. I tried to pull away, but he had me in a headlock. "Don't screw it up."

I shoved him off and considered suffocating him with his half-eaten sandwich, but that'd be a waste of good food. "We should bury your ass."

Chapter Twenty-Nine

Frida and Granma were arguing about the benefits of lemon water and if it helps you lose weight. Frida had her doubts, but Granma was determined it did and would drink it for the next few months in preparation for her wedding day. Somewhere in Mombasa, I imagined our ancestors turning in their graves at the idea of one of them wanting to lose weight.

I hesitated a moment before I stepped into the kitchen, a bit uneasy at seeing Frida, especially so soon after waking up when my brain was still operating irrationally—Frida and I weren't in a war zone anymore. She glanced up and gave me a nod, pointed to the pancakes she was making, and asked if I wanted some. Hell, yes, I did. I had to admit, whatever Frida cooked usually melted in my mouth. Granma started the fancy coffee maker Paul had bought and retreated to her room, leaving Frida and me alone.

This was the first time since the talk we'd had last week that it was only us in the room—without Paul cutting through the awkward with numerous questions about

Frida's production work, or Granma talking about random stuff like how toothpaste could cause cancer.

I hadn't been ignoring her, not consciously at least. There'd been lots of homework, sending out applications, and studying. And on top of all that, hanging out with Adam, which involved a lot of tongue action and teeth, but only when the twins weren't present. Otherwise, we'd snuggled together as we watched TV. It'd been nice. It only made me want to ask him to be my boyfriend even more.

Frida put the last of the pancakes on a plate and carried the pan to the sink. By an unspoken agreement, we'd gone on with our lives as if the conversation hadn't happened—that was okay with me; I had clarity now. I think the awkwardness was because, even with that talk out of the way, we were still not familiar with each other. But it was less of a burden to say "hi" because, sometimes, I didn't have to say it, Frida did.

"Smoothie?" Frida pointed at the slimy brown and green stuff she was now pouring into a glass.

I fought back my gag reflex. "No thanks."

"It's good for your joints."

"I'm pretty sure I have a decade or two before I start worrying about such stuff."

A moment later, the door to Granma's room opened, and Paul walked out humming a Billy Ocean song Granma liked. He noticed us staring and greeted us cheerily, the smile on his face only growing wider, and stepped into the bathroom.

"That's not weird to you?" Frida asked.

"It's so weird; I try not to think about it." I drizzled syrup on my pancakes. "I thought you didn't notice."

"Oh, I notice." She shrugged. "But he's alright."

"I guess." I took my plate and headed for the living room. I plopped down on the sofa and reached into my pocket to pull out my phone. There was a text from Adam asking if I was still going over—hell yes—and another from Tani, showing how her pink collection was growing.

Frida leaned against the wall, the glass with the gross stuff in her hand, and her eyes fixed on me.

"What?" I asked.

"I, uh, saw a therapist on Wednesday."

"Oh."

"If you're interested in seeing one; let me know."

"I will."

*

The offer consumed my brain as I biked it to Adam's place. Did I want to see a therapist? A professional at handling human emotions and trauma? Someone who I wouldn't have to see every day. Someone who wouldn't judge. Yes. I wanted to.

Em was the one who opened the door with a heavy sigh. "No more diving, okay? We've moved on to something else."

"Oh, what?"

"Knitting."

I laughed and stepped into the house. "Knitting?"

"We get to sit down and watch TV while we do it."

"And eat," Maya said as she wrapped herself around me in a hug. I patted her back. She was as affectionate as Adam, if not more. "You can join us if you want. We'll be watching YouTube tutorials."

"Learn to knit?" I asked. That one thing that had never crossed my mind before, and the only people I'd seen knitting were old ladies from old movies.

"He's totally having sexist thoughts, isn't he?" Em stage-whispered.

"No, I'm not." I kind of was thinking that. But most worrying was the age thing and sitting there with my thoughts. I didn't think so.

"I can see it," Maya hissed.

I rolled my eyes. "I'm not." I'd just rather be making out with Adam.

Maya pouted. "He was totally using us to get to Adam."

Em frowned, and in one blink, her eyes became misty. "I thought we were friends."

I fidgeted in alarm. "We're friends, definitely—"

"Then why can't we knit together?" Maya asked, sniffling.

Someone help me. This was emotional blackmail. I could smell it. I opened my mouth to tell them to knock it off but made the mistake of looking at their faces, wide eyes, and dimpled cheeks. "Fine, we can knit."

Maya squealed in delight and hugged me again.

"Meet you upstairs," Em called as she headed for the kitchen.

"Blackmail is illegal, you know," I told Maya.

"You'll love it!" I highly doubt that. "You can knit Adam a scarf with the colors of the bisexual flag."

"We'll see... Is he here?"

"Not home yet; now come on." Maya grabbed my arm and led me up the stairs.

Knitting was chaotic. There were huffs of frustration, a bit of screaming from Em's end when she couldn't get the needles and yarn to cooperate, nonstop complaining from me, shrills of joy from Maya, who caught on fast, and watching a kids' drama where a girl named Lilly hadn't sent a birthday invite to another girl. I liked it better this way; I didn't get to think.

When we went downstairs in search of a cold drink, we found Mr. Herman in the kitchen making supper. The girls leaned over the stove, eager to see what was cooking, and he started to grill me about school. When Adam walked in, my heart fluttered. I wanted to go up to him and pull him into a tight hug, then kiss him so hard he went dizzy. I hadn't seen him since Friday, and, yes, I was needy for his affection. I settled for a grin, contented when he grinned back. The smile faltered when he saw his dad.

Adam walked past me as he headed for the fridge and let his fingers run down my back as he did. I straightened as heat flooded the back of my neck. He grabbed an apple and came to stand close to me, our arms and thighs brushing.

"Are you two together?" Mr. Herman asked quietly. We both froze, and the twins' chatter died. I bristled. His dark eyebrows and those hazel-brown eyes always made him look intimidating, and this was no exception.

"Umm." My mouth opened and closed like a fish.

"No..." Adam stammered.

"You think I was born yesterday?" Mr. Herman said with a laugh.

"Uh..." Adam fidgeted, and my whole body burned with heat. Adam opened his mouth to say something but snapped it shut.

"I didn't say it, but I do accept you and support that you are bisexual. Alright?" Adam nodded slowly. "Point is, if you and Rasheed are dating, I'm fine with it. And you don't have to hide it for my sake, though we'll have to talk about it later."

Natalie came in and noticed our shaken expressions. "Now what did you do to these boys, Michael?"

Mr. Herman laughed. "Why do you always make me out to be the bad guy? I asked them if they're together."

Natalie's eyes widened with amusement. "Are you?"

"No."

She arched an eyebrow. "Really?"

"We've not discussed it yet, alright?" Adam said.

"Alright, no need for that tone."

When we got back to Adam's room, I hovered by the door. I had to do it now. This was the perfect opportunity.

"What?" Adam asked when he noticed me frozen there.

God. I'd never done this in person, only over text. The distance a safety net. I'd faced Frida and a wronged ex. I could do this.

"I know I don't have the best track record for relationships," I said.

"You're eighteen," Adam pointed out.

"I know, but it was still wrong, the way I treated Scott, and I'm trying to be self-aware."

Adam chewed his lip and bounced his gaze around the room before he settled on me, forehead a little creased. He had to know what was coming next. Shit, what if he didn't want a relationship? I would survive, I assured myself. It would suck and be very awkward, but I'd survive.

I swallowed the fears and pushed on. "I know you mentioned not wanting to date, but I'd like to be your boyfriend. I like you...a lot. I want to do it with you and do it right." I wouldn't screw it up. "You know, go out as a couple, and hold hands. That kind of stuff... But if you're not ready, that's umm...fine, no pressure, and if you are but don't want to tell everyone, that's fine too." I fidgeted. "And take your time thinking on it. I can be, maybe, a handful."

"You're okay," Adam said with a tight-lipped smile.

I laughed. "Well, to let you know—liking someone can overwhelm me, and I might pull away, and you might have to pull me back."

"Understood."

"Oh, and we don't have to fill our social media with pictures of us, and we can skip the matching outfits, I guess." Okay, now I was rambling.

He rubbed his face and groaned. "I can't believe I thought matching outfits were okay."

"I thought it was cute." My muscles relaxed at the new direction the conversation was taking, enough that I could take the steps to sit next to Adam, with an inch of space between us. "There's that one where you and Sarah had matching sweaters and blue jeans; it was cute. You looked so good in yellow."

"I hate yellow," he said vehemently.

"Wow, okay, then I can't hang out with you anymore," I teased.

"But it's yellow! It's so bright and in your face."

"And warm. And pretty."

"See, here's another reason not to like it—it's causing a divide between us."

"Well, another benefit of being boyfriends is there's an option to agree to disagree." My cheeks flushed. I hoped I wasn't overselling and pressuring.

Adam reached for my hand, turned it so the palm was facing up, and slid his hand into it. "I like you, too, Rasheed."

My breath hitched. "Yeah."

"And I'd like to be your boyfriend."

I laughed in delight and bent down for a kiss.

Epilogue

Granma stopped crying only when it was time to eat. She'd cried the moment Babu Rasheed hooked her left arm in his and when I took her right arm as we prepared to walk down the aisle. She'd cried as Pastor Obinna—the head of the African Church—had read their vows. She'd been incoherent during the signing of the marriage certificate. Good thing Natalie had thought to bring tissues, which Granma quickly went through.

Paul smiled the entire ceremony, which amused me and cemented my belief that he had the best intentions for Granma—seriously, how were his cheeks not hurting?

The reception happened in the Mayflower Hotel. It was set up in simple fashion, no large centerpieces, only a formal table arrangement, a few flowers, and a buffet. The attendance was small, mostly people from church, a portion of the Herman clan, and a few family members—Babu Rasheed, his wife, and two cousins.

After they'd eaten, Paul and Granma had their first dance to "At Last" by Etta James. It mortified me seeing

Paul and Granma dance so close. I sighed when the song faded out, and the DJ switched to some late-eighties soul music. I danced with Granma next, to Whitney's "I'll Always Love You," which was very relevant.

"Glad you finally stopped crying."

"Oh stop." She huffed. She was radiant in a bright-yellow patterned *kitenge*—chosen because she reasoned she could wear it more than once and remember her wedding day. Flowered henna designs covered her hands and legs, and she was smiling brightly.

"I'm happy for you Granma."

She sniffed. "Don't make me cry again."

"But I am. I wanted you to know."

"*Asante*. Are you sure you don't want to join us in Mombasa?"

"I'm sure. I'll go another time."

For their honeymoon, Granma and Paul would vacation in Mombasa, and sure, okay, I missed the place, but there was no way I'd know peace if I had a constant reminder that they shared a bed. Thank the heavens I was going to college. I was also glad Paul would be there to keep her company.

The song ended, and when the music changed to late-2000 R and B, the small dance floor flooded with more people. Paul snagged Granma from me.

"Take care of her," I said to him.

"You know I will."

Tani grabbed my hand and pulled me onto the floor before I could go search for Adam. We'd not had a moment longer than five seconds together, but I could never say no to Rihanna.

From the dance floor, I saw Frida standing by the buffet table with a glass in hand, pretty in a red-and-black *kitenge* dress. She had a wide-eyed expression like someone had dragged her here by her feet. She startled when she noticed my gaze on her and then raised her glass in salute. I nodded in acknowledgment. She had stayed after all. The only time she'd been away recently was the two weeks at the beginning of December when she needed to sort out work stuff, but she had come back.

Sauti Sol and Alikiba's "Unconditionally Bae" started playing, and the song's first line struck a chord in me. The song spoke of love being essential. My eyes quickly scanned the crowd for Adam. He sat next to Mo— a new anime had dropped, and they couldn't shut up about it. I vibrated with joy when he looked up, and our eyes snagged. He stood and made his way toward me. My heart leaped in excitement.

"Okay," Tani said, dragging the vowels. "I'll go beg Peep to dance with me."

That, I would have paid to see, but I couldn't drag my eyes from Adam, who wore a tailored black suit that fit him like a glove.

"Hey," he said.

"Hi," I said, taking his hand. "Want to dance?"

"I'd love to, though I'm not sure I can do anything energetic." He pointed at his brand-new leather shoes. "They're killing me."

"We can take it slow." I wrapped my arms around his waist, pulled him against me, and rested my head on his shoulder. "I'll also hold you tight until you mostly forget about it."

He snuggled closer. "Sounds perfect."

It was. With his heart beating in sync with mine, music and laughter mingled in the background, and joy flooded my chest.

Glossary of Swahili Terms

Vocabulary:

ACHARI — a snack made from thin slices of dried mango, dipped in a mixture of red food coloring, sugar, and chili.

AMKA — awake

BABU — grandfather

BABU KACHRI — a very popular street food in Mombasa, Kenya, consisting of a thick, tangy potato gravy sprinkled with crushed potato crisps, and *khara sev* (a fried crispy snack made from chickpea flour and spices), and topped with a spicy chutney

CASSAVA — any of several plants having fleshy rootstocks yieldng a nutritious starch and cultivated throughout the tropics, providing a staple food

DERA — a loose cotton dress

JAMHURI DAY — (Republic Day) a Kenyan national holiday celebrated on 12 December each year

JINIS — evil spirits

KACHRI — a vegetable (wild melon) used as a spice in Indian cuisine

KACHRI BATETA — (commonly known as Babu Kachri) a popular street food in Mombasa; a light potato stew with sour green mangoes, topped with fresh coconut and fried cassava crisps

KITENGE — a colorful African fabric similar to a sarong, often worn by women and wrapped around the chest or waist, over the head as a headscarf, or as a baby sling

KOLACHE — a bun made of rich, sweet yeast-leavened dough filled with jam or fruit pulp; originally from Eastern Europe

KUMBE — "Oh." An interjection used when there's a revelation.

MAHAMRI — Swahili for a sweet cardamom-spiced bread or bun made with coconut milk powder

MATATU — privately owned minibus

MJIBAMBE — slang for "have fun"

NYANYA — grandmother

PEPO CHAFU — evil spirits

PILIPILI NA NDIMU — peppers and lemons

POLE — sorry

PWEZA — octopus

RAHA — enjoyment, ease

SEV — a popular Indian snack food consisting of small pieces of crunchy noodles made from chickpea flour paste, seasoned with turmeric, cayenne, and *ajwain* (a herb cultivated in Indian and Iran), and deep fried in oil

TAARAB — from the Arabic for "having joy with music," a genre of music common on the East African coast.

UGALI — a type of maize flour mush; popular in East Africa

UNDUGU — brotherhood

ZILE SIMU ZA TELKOM — Telkom phones

ZILIZOPENDWA — literally, "those which were loved," a term used in Kenya to refer to early Kenyan popular music, synonymous with the term "golden oldies" in the US

Phrases:

ANAJARIBU KUNIUA. — He's trying to kill me.

ASANTE — Thank you

EH, MNANIONAJE? — How do I look?

KUKIWA NA SHIDA, KULA KWANZA. — If there is a problem, eat first.

KWENI UNAHAMA NA SIJUI? — You are moving out, and I do not know?

MAAJABU YA MUSA — the wonders of Moses

MAJI YAKIMWAGIKA HAYAZOLEKI. — Water under the bridge.

MI NA PAUL TUMEAMUA KUFUNGA NDOA. — Paul and I have decided that we will get married.

MTOTO WA NYOKA NI NYOKA. — (a proverb) An apple doesn't fall far from the tree

NENDA KAMLETEE GLASI YA MAJI. — Go get him a glass of water.

NIMEDANGANYA? — Have I lied?

SASA UNAENDA WAPI? — Where are you going now?

TAFADHALI — Please

TAFADHALI AMKA. — Please get up.

TUMBO LAKO LITAFURA. — Your stomach will swell.

UJUE NAKUPENDA. — Know that I love you.

ULIKUWA MDOGO. — You were young.

USIKATE CARROT ZIWE KUBWA HIVYO. — Do not cut the carrots so large.

USITUME NIKWAMBIE MARA YA PILI. — Don't make me ask again.

UTAJUTA — You will regret it.

WALI WA NAZI NA UROJO. — Coconut rice and *urojo*. (*Urojo*, also known as "Zanzibar street mix," is a colorful stew of potatoes and chickpea flour noodles in a soup stock that perfectly captures Swahili culture.)

Acknowledgements

Thank you, Elizabetta, my editor, for picking this one and for everything else in between.

Thank you, Mom, for being supportive of my weird endeavours, and Shosh for teaching me patience and resilience.

Thank you, Kinyoi, for being the first person I met who understands depression and the first to read my stuff (without permission btw). Thank you, Kelvin, for not giving up on me and listening to my rants.

Thank you, Allan, for calling to ask if I was done (I am now, for real this time). Thank you, baby bro, for asking if all I do is type-type (it seems so).

And thank you so much, Linda, for the laughs (I was losing my mind) and for hoping I'll be the next Chimamanda even though all I want to write about is people kissing...a lot.

About A. Aduma

Aduma is an economics major at the University of Nairobi in Kenya, and the type of person who feels incomplete without a book in hand. When not reading or writing, Aduma can be found lost in spreadsheets and graphs with music for company.

Twitter:
@Ballardofme

Also from NineStar Press

I Knew Him by Abigail de Niverville

In his senior year of high school, Julian has one goal: be invisible. All he wants is to study hard, play basketball, and pretend he's straight for one more year. Then, he can run away to university and finally tell the world he's bisexual. And by "the world," he means everyone but his mom and best friend. That's two conversations he never wants to have.

When he's talked into auditioning for the school's production of *Hamlet*, Julian fears that veering off course will lead to assumptions he's not ready to face. Despite that, he can't help but feel a connection to this play. His absent father haunts him like a ghost, his ex is being difficult, and he's overthinking everything. It's driving him crazy.

The decision to audition leads Julian on an entirely different path. He's cast as Hamlet, and the boy playing Horatio is unlike anyone Julian has met before. Mysterious and flirtatious, Sky draws Julian in, even though he fears his feelings at the same time. As the two grow closer, Julian begins to let out the secrets he's never told—the ones that have paralyzed him for years. But what will he do if Sky feels the same way?

We Go Together by Abigail de Niverville

The beaches of Grand-Barachois had been Kat's summer home for years. There, she created her own world with her "summer friends," full of possibilities and free from expectation. But one summer, everything changed, and she ran from the life she'd created.

Now seventeen and on the brink of attending college, Kat is full of regret. She's broken a friendship beyond repair, and she's dated possibly the worst person in the world. Six months after their break-up, he still haunts her nightmares. Confused and scared, she returns to Grand-Barachois to sort out her feelings.

When she arrives, everything is different yet familiar. Some of her friends are right where she left them, while some are nowhere to be found. There are so many things they never got to do, so many words left unsaid.

And then there's Tristan.

He wasn't supposed to be there. He was just a guy from Kat's youth orchestra days. When the two meet again, they become fast friends. Tristan has a few ideas to make this summer the best one yet. Together, they build a master list of all the things Kat and her friends wanted to do but never could. It's finally time to live their wildest childhood dreams.

But the past won't let Kat go. And while this may be a summer to remember, there's so much she wants to forget.

Bigger Love by Rick R. Reed

Truman Reid is Summitville High's most out-and-proud senior. He can't wait to take his fierce, uncompromising self away from his small Ohio River hometown, where he's suffered more than his share of bullying. He's looking forward to bright lights and a big city. Maybe he'll be the first ever genderfluid star to win an Academy Award. But all that changes on the first day of school when he locks eyes with the most gorgeous hunk he's ever seen.

Mike Stewart, big, dark-haired, and with the most amazing blue eyes, is new to town. He's quiet, manly, and has the sexy air of a lost soul. It's almost love at first sight for Truman. He thinks that love could deepen when Mike becomes part of the stage crew for Harvey, the senior class play Truman's directing. But is Mike even gay? And how will it work when Truman's mother is falling for Mike's dad?

Plus Truman, never the norm, makes a daring and controversial choice for the production that has the whole town up in arms.

See how it all plays out on a stage of love, laughter, tears, and sticking up for one's essential self...

Connect with NineStar Press

www.ninestarpress.com

www.facebook.com/ninestarpress

www.facebook.com/groups/NineStarNiche

www.twitter.com/ninestarpress

www.instagram.com/ninestarpress